Unlikely Soldiers Book Four
(Murder and Mayhem)
By Deb McEwan

Cover Design by Jessica Bell

In loving memory of
Marjorie Groves
21st October 1934 to 20th September 2019
forever in our hearts
Brian, Steven and Debbie
x

Chapter 1 – 2 Years after Guy's Death

It was pitch black as Mouse dreamily opened one eye and smiled. She turned over, still expecting to feel Guy's arm slip around her waist and his warmth flood her body.

Her smile disappeared as she remembered he was dead. Gone. Cremated. Dust to dust and all that.

'Noooooo,' she screamed as the reality of the cruel dream sank in, and then she howled like a wounded animal as the pain hit first her heart and then her brain. Mouse continued to howl until banging on the wall stopped her.

A few seconds later there was a knock on the door.

'Do you want to talk, love?'

'No thanks, I'm fine.' Mouse cringed after saying the words-she'd heard that some transit personnel were going to stay in the Sergeants Mess but didn't know they'd moved in that day. The RSM's policy was to keep transit visitors and permanent staff separate but a few of the blocks were being renovated so the visitors had to be accommodated in the spare rooms, usually reserved for permanent staff.

'You're clearly not. I'm a Welfare Worker and can help you.'

Shit that was all she needed! 'I'm fine. Really,' she called through the closed door. 'Sorry for disturbing you, it won't happen again.'

'But...'

'Sorry again. I'll let you get back to sleep now.'

Mouse waited a few moments but there was no response. Sitting up in bed, she hugged her knees to her chest, then as the tears began once more, put her head onto her knees and sobbed quietly. It seemed like an age before she was able to bring herself back under control, and when she did, curled up into the foetal position, totally exhausted.

Despite her fatigue, she was still upset, and Guy's death felt as raw as it had from the beginning. How could this be after two years? Fed up with tossing and turning, she decided to make a mug of hot chocolate in the Mess Kitchen.

She quickly dressed and tiptoed to the bathroom. After using the loo, she splashed cold water over her face in the hope it would reduce the puffiness. A few minutes later she left her accommodation block and began heading for the main mess building which housed the kitchen, dining room and public areas. It had just turned 4 o'clock and was too early for any of the morning staff to be on duty, and too late for the night-time shift. She shone her torch light on the Simplex lock on the door, keyed in the number and opened the door when she heard the click of the locking mechanism. After the brightness of the outside security light the darkness inside was almost palpable. Mouse remembered briefly how she used to be frightened when entering a dark and empty building. That was before her life had become a tragedy, and now the worst had happened, she didn't give a shit.

She would soon rediscover some of her fears.

Mouse opened the dining room door and shone her torch towards the wall so she could see the light switch. As the light from the torch hit the floor, she did a double take, initially believing her brain had deceived her. She took a huge breath then slowly swung the light back onto the floor.

'Jesus effing Christ!'

Unable to take her eyes off the body in front of her, Mouse ran the torchlight the length of the man and noticed the large puddle of blood on the left side of his torso.

'Get a grip, woman,' she muttered to herself as she shone the torch to the wall and rushed over to hit the light switch. The scene was even more macabre in the bright light. Knowing deep in her gut that the man was no longer alive – his brown eyes were open and his face an ashen grey – she also knew she had to check to be sure.

As she stared at the man, she realised he was someone she knew. 'Chinese Pete.' Mouse spoke out loud again as she rushed over to him and knelt down at his side, managing to avoid some of the blood. After checking his wrist there was no pulse as she had suspected, and the body of Chinese Pete was already cold. As she gently laid his arm back down, she noticed the tattoo on the underside, further up his wrist which showed the number 14 in a small circle and Chinese writing. Mouse wondered what it symbolized. Shaking her head, she got to her feet and ran to the phone in the hallway. She dialled the civvy emergency services first, knowing she'd probably get a bollocking off someone for doing so. Her second call was to the military police station. When the junior rank on duty answered the phone and Mouse explained what had happened, he was initially slow to take details. She told him the Civvy Police were on their way and his attitude changed.

'I'll get onto the boss straight away, Sergeant Halfpenny. Remain where you are.'

'Of course,' she replied deciding not to make any sarcastic comments. He sounded quite young, so this was probably the most important thing he'd had to deal with so far in his career.

Her next call was to the Duty Officer in the Big House, Headquarters British Army of the Rhine. Mouse calmly explained what she'd discovered and suggested to the young captain that he may want to contact Chief G1, Media Ops, as well as the Military Assistant to the General.

'I don't need you to tell me how to do my job and who I need to speak to, Sergeant Halfpenny.'

'I know you don't, Sir, but you need to know that I'm keeping a record of my actions to assist the police with their enquiries and to ensure that our seniors have an idea of the timeline. It's always useful, Sir, in case anything hits the fan. I'll let you get on now.'

'Ah, thank you, Sergeant Halfpenny, point taken.'

Mouse hung up the phone, feeling smug despite the tragic circumstances.

Her smugness left her as the WRAC RSM who had a military phone in her room answered her next call, on the eleventh ring.

'It's Sergeant Halfpenny, Ma'am.'

'Why are you calling me at this hour? What's happened? This had better be good Sergeant...'

'I found Chinese Pete in the dining room, Ma'am. He's dead.' Mouse let the words sink in for a few seconds.

'What...? Mr Wong?'

'Yes, Ma'am. He's dead. I've informed the civvy police, RMP and headquarters duty officer,' she paused as the sound of sirens neared.

'Why didn't you call me first?' Not waiting for an answer, the RSM added, 'I'm on my way.' Then she hung up.

*****

Mouse was interviewed by the civilian police and the Special Investigation Branch of the Royal Military Police who remained with her while the civilian police concluded their part of the interview. Guy's old boss, Warrant Officer Class One Wardson was due for a posting in a few weeks, but he was still the SIB RSM and made the whole process less stressful than it could have been. If it hadn't been for her connection through marriage, Mouse would have felt the same about the SIB as all the other soldiers – that they thought you were guilty of a crime, even if you were the one who had reported it and were simply a witness or an innocent bystander.

She was told she could leave but being intrinsically curious she hung around and eavesdropped where she could. She overheard the SIB RSM and a civilian policeman.

'Could be Triad related,' said the RSM.

'God I hope not...' the civvy responded before a colleague approached him and he wandered off. She had decided she would go to the office early, but now the SIB RSM was alone. Knowing he would treat her kindly because of Guy, Mouse approached him.

'Triads, Sir?'

'Chinese Mafia, Mouse. We suspect that Peter Wong was connected...'

'The show's over Sergeant Halfpenny,' the WRAC RSM called as she approached them both. 'Get yourself off to work and if the police need to speak to you again, I'll let you know.'

Guy's RSM gave her a sympathetic look and she rolled her eyes at him, out of sight of her own RSM.

'Look after yourself, Mouse. Guy's friends and RMP family are still here if you need us.'

'Thanks, Sir.' She knew they were only words, but it was still good of them to think of her. Her own RSM was waiting patiently, not saying a word, which was most unusual for her, Mouse thought.

'And remember that life goes on never mind how hard. He wouldn't have wanted your life to end when his did. Try to move on now.'

Nobody referred directly to the meltdown she'd had following Guy's death. She was over that part of the grief now, but some still didn't know how to act around her. She smiled briefly not bothering to say she felt that her life had ended when Guy's did, and left without another word.

*****

As she suspected, Mouse received a bollocking for calling the civilian police before the military police, but it blew over the following day. When the admin staff had typed up her statement, she was called in to read it and certify that it was an accurate description of what happened when she found Chinese Pete, and what she had told the police. Mouse signed and dated it.

'Can I see the RSM?' she asked the duty sergeant in the hope she could get further information about the case and to thank him again for his support.

The sergeant looked surprised but he picked up the phone. After a brief conversation he turned to Mouse and said. 'He's not available at the moment. Why do you want to see him?'

Mouse pursed her lips. She didn't want to explain she knew the RSM through Guy because she didn't know the duty sergeant and was fed up with the awkwardness of people every time she told them what had happened. Saying that, the Royal Military Police were a small Corps and she had no doubt this man knew what had happened to Guy despite the passing of time, but he didn't know that she was Guy's widow.

'It doesn't matter. I'll speak to him another time.'

'If you have any information that could help with the enquiry...'

'It's nothing like that,' Mouse interrupted. 'I'll be on my way.'

The duty sergeant watched her leave. 'That's her isn't it?' he said to the man in the suit who had come to collect the envelope containing the statement Mouse had signed. His colleague nodded. 'Yup. Poor cow, eh?'

The duty sergeant nodded in agreement then got on with his work. At least the killer of Sergeant Guy Halfpenny had received his just desserts, and his accomplice had received a dishonourable discharge and was deservedly rotting away in civvy nick.

That was more than could be said for the killer of Chinese Pete whose death would open a can of worms that would spread to another part of the world.

*****

Three weeks later the new captain in the directorate called Mouse in for a career chat. Mouse was looking forward to the chat - ever since the discovery of Chinese Pete she'd been playing the 'what if' game. What if she moved on? What if she left Germany? What if people thought she was running away from Guy's memory? What if she could never move on with her life? She had remained in the WRAC Directorate since Guy's death and despite all of the 'what if's', felt that now was the time for pastures new. She had itchy feet and was ready to move. No matter how long she remained in JHQ, the memories would always be too painful, and she didn't feel she could move on with her life until she moved location.

'The colonel wants me to speak to you about your posting request Sergeant Halfpenny. She's happy for you to stay here longer, amongst people you know.'

'The colonel does know that I'm not ten years old, Ma'am, doesn't she? And that I am the best person to decide what is best for me?'

'I'm sure she does, Sergeant Halfpenny.' There was a flicker of amusement in Captain Longthorn's eyes and Mouse was beginning to realise this new officer wasn't as naive as some of the senior ranks in the Sergeants Mess made her out to be.

'And what do you think, Ma'am?'

'I think you are still grieving, Sergeant Halfpenny. We don't always make the right decisions when we've lost a loved one and I wonder if enough time has passed for you to...'

'But it's been two years...'

'Let me finish, please.' It was said in a polite, courteous manner and silenced Mouse. 'I also happen to think you know your own mind and it would be good if you could be in Hong Kong with your brother and his wife.'

'I sense a 'but', Ma'am,' said Mouse. She didn't want the newbie captain to think she could have it all her own way.

'I'm a career officer, Sergeant Halfpenny. I'm not in to find myself a husband then become a baby-making machine. So, I have to be seen to carry out the will of the colonel and if she wants to keep you here...'

'Damn!' said Mouse. So the colonel had decided this newbie captain was going to give her the bad news. This woman who was playing around with the ADC and didn't know that it was one of the main topics around the dining table in the Sergeants Mess.

'So, Ma'am. Does the colonel know that you're planning a full career? If she's aware of...' Mouse stopped herself mid-sentence but they both knew what she was about to say.

'Yes, I do enjoy the company of the general's aide de camp and the colonel seems to think it's serious which suits me for now. And speaking of Captain Todd,' she added. 'he's a font of information.' She had a twinkle in her eyes and Mouse knew she was waiting for her to ask what Captain Todd had told her. She didn't take the bait and Captain Longthorn was the first to cave. 'He was talking to me earlier about the Deputy Commander of the British Forces in Hong Kong, Brigadier Harding-Brown, who just happens to be his uncle.' She had Mouse's full attention now and carried on. 'Apparently the brigadier will be looking for a new PA in the not too distant future but is looking for a trained shorthand writer who are few and far between these days, or so I'm told.'

'Ah, I see.'

'So how do you feel about doing a three-month shorthand writer's course at Worthy Down?'

'Seriously, Ma'am?'

'Yes, seriously. Then if the posting does come up, at least you'll be qualified. And if it doesn't, it's another string to your bow, so to speak.'

'Do you think you'll be able to sell it to the colonel?'

'With a little help from my friends, let's just say there's a good chance.'

Chapter 2 – Sowing the Seeds

The boss called her into her office the following day. Major Best, her former boss and Major Drake – her officer commanding and Major Best's partner - had supported Captain Longthorn, agreeing that it was time for Mouse to move on. Between them they had managed to convince the colonel it was the right decision and the colonel had eventually agreed. The fact that Mouse was the best Chief Clerk she ever had made it hard work for the other officers, but the colonel knew deep down that it was in Sergeant Halfpenny's best interests to move on now.

Mouse had seen a number of changes while doing the job in the Women's Royal Army Corps Directorate, including the routine arming of female soldiers. The WRAC was changing. Most of the young female soldiers Mouse met were enthusiastic and ready for change, but there were also many older soldiers who were resistant, and she wondered what the future held for them. For her part she was ready for something new and decided to embrace whatever the future held. She was desperate to get away, believing that distance and a fresh start might dull the pain that was still like a dagger slicing through her heart. Even though she didn't cry every day now, it was still a struggle to get through without doing so or screaming at the injustices of life.

For the first time since Guy's death there was a dim light at the end of the tunnel. She was told she was one of an elite group *specially selected* to attend the three-month shorthand writer's course at Worthy Down, the new clerical training school now that Deepcut had been taken over by the Royal Army Ordnance Corps, and she could then expect to work in a PA role to senior officers, subject to passing this course. She was the only one taking the course so knew there'd be nowhere to hide, and she'd have to knuckle down.

The tears flowed freely when Mouse said goodbye to Major Best with promises that they'd always stay in touch, but as she left the camp in the transport to the airport, a sense of relief swept over her and lifted the tightness in her chest. It would be some time before she could smile at the memories of good times with Guy, and she knew that the memory of his murder and that of their adorable dog, Becks, would always be emblazoned into her mind.

Living in the Sergeants Mess in Worthy Down, Mouse mostly kept to herself. A couple of weeks into the training she overheard two mess members talking about her and the general consensus appeared to be that she was stuck up and up herself. Mouse shrugged. She didn't particularly care what others thought-they hadn't lived her life so could go fuck themselves as far as she was concerned.

At weekends she either studied or went to visit her parents – anything but spend too much time alone with her thoughts.

In the final month of the three-month course Mouse was called into the Admin Officer's office and given some news.

'The Deputy Commander PA post isn't available just now, Sergeant Halfpenny. You'll have to wait your turn.'

She wasn't bothered if it was just a hiccup. A few weeks or a month was not a problem and Mouse told him so. 'I've lots of leave left so maybe I could take that while I'm waiting, Sir?'

He laughed. 'I doubt that very much. She's been extended in post so we're talking one to two years, Sergeant Halfpenny.'

'One to two years, Sir? But why can't I go and do a different job. You know I'm an experienced administrator and can turn my hand to any role.'

'And that's exactly what I want to speak to you about now,' he replied. 'Due to your skills and flexibility we have something a bit different for you.'

Her bullshit-ometer went off the scale as Mouse sat down and listened to the Admin Officer. 'As soon as you finish your course you're off to the Ministry of Defence in London. The civvy PA who works for the Director of Public relations has been headhunted and is leaving. You've been specially selected for this job which could be the making of you, Sergeant Halfpenny.'

Specially selected, my arse, thought Mouse. *More likely they couldn't find another sucker willing to do the job without a fuss so I've been volunteered for it.* She could think of worse places to go than London but was hugely disappointed as it didn't hold a candle to the thought of a posting to Hong Kong. Mouse had been counting on Hong Kong as being the panacea she needed and now that wasn't going to happen.

*****

Mouse had four days before she had to report for duty, so she planned to spend some time with Elaine. Jill had died before Guy and Mouse felt Elaine was the only one who truly knew what it was like to lose the love of your life. Feeling restless while on leave at her parents', she decided on impulse to go to Elaine's a day early. Knowing that her best friend wouldn't mind, she didn't phone, deciding instead to surprise her. She knocked on the door.

'Here's the pizzas.'

The voice from inside was familiar but it wasn't Elaine's. By the time her brain had worked it out the door was open, and they were staring at each other.

'Bloody hell! Spike! What are you doing here? Great to see you.' Mouse hugged her old roomie from her early days in JHQ. Spike was enthusiastic in returning the embrace, but Mouse sensed some discomfort and knew something was going on. Her feelings were confirmed after she hugged Elaine and both her friends avoided eye contact.

'How long?'

'What do you mean, Mouse?' said Spike.

'It's no good, Spike. She knows.'

'Look, do you want me to go tonight?'

'No.' Mouse and Elaine both said at the same time.

'Don't go on my account, I'll find somewhere else to stay,' Mouse continued.

'No need, Mouse. Spike's leaving tomorrow and I was going to tell you before you left for London because I didn't

11

want your visit to be about me and Spike. If I'd known you were arriving today…' Her voice trailed off.

Mouse frowned. *How long had this been going on?*

Spike seemed to read her mind. 'It's early days yet. And we're taking it slowly. I'm not trying to replace Jill. Nobody could do that.'

'But it has been nearly two and a half years, Mouse, and Jill would want me to move on.'

They seemed to be seeking her approval somehow. 'It's none of my business. I know only too well that you have to find happiness wherever you can.'

'So you don't mind then?'

'Of course not, Elaine. It was a surprise, but I get that was my fault for trying to surprise you. Shall I sleep on the sofa tonight?'

'Err, no need,' said Elaine. 'The spare room is free.'

Spike looked like a teenager who had just been caught at it by her parents and Mouse burst into laughter; Her friends joined her.

Later, when they'd reminisced about the good times and eaten and drunk their fill, Elaine tried to broach the subject of Mouse dating again. Mouse bit her head off.

'No way Elaine, It's not going to happen. Never!'

If Elaine was surprised by her friend's outburst, she didn't mention it again.

*****

It was day one of the new job and as she got on the rickety Northern Line underground train at stupid o'clock in the morning, she wondered what she'd let herself in for. The train was shabby, stank of smoke and was badly in need of refurbishment. It looked like something left over from World War Two. But what was worse than the state of the train, was the man who'd got on at Finchley Central and had decided to sit opposite her. She tried to avoid eye contact with him as he was making suggestive gestures towards her. Looking around, it felt like all the nutters often found in cities congregated on this line so that commuters on other routes could have a more pleasant journey. She figured this one was in his late twenties when he leered at her when they'd briefly made eye contact. He then grabbed hold of his balls and gave them a suggestive shake. Refusing to be outwardly intimidated she remained seated, though she did a mental calculation about the distance from her seat to the door and Mouse reckoned she could reach it, and the emergency bell, before him if he did decide to make a grab for her. Hopefully, if push came to shove, one of the other commuters on the train would help out. She wasn't sure about that though as she'd heard stories of people hiding behind their papers, books, or pretending to be asleep when others had been attacked. *Spineless bastards,* she thought before reminding herself to rein in her overactive imagination.

Thankfully, he got off at Camden Town without further incident and she tried to concentrate on thoughts of her new job.

Alighting the rickety old train at Embankment, Mouse figured that outside of work London was not exactly going to be a barrel of laughs. The Sergeants' Mess accommodation was in the Postal Depot in Mill Hill so she would be subjected to this tedious daily commute. However, the short walk to her new workplace invigorated her, even though it was through central London.

Mouse was chuffed that she'd managed to navigate her way to Main Building without any issues. It was only a short five-minute walk but with her renowned disastrous sense of direction, nothing short of amazing that she got there without diversion. She looked up at the imposing dirty white building. The Ministry of Defence was going to be a whole new experience. Having worked at unit and divisional level, she now had the opportunity to discover how the decisions of policy makers impacted those below them and she intended to suck up as much information as she could. The Civil Servant who had worked as PA to the Director of Publications (Army) had taken a much better paid job in the City, so Mouse was a temporary stand-in until they found a suitable civilian replacement. She believed the job would suit her nosey nature as she would hear about events as they were happening; many of interest to the wider public that would appear in the country's media.

She took a deep breath and walked in. There was double security in this building and, after walking into the outer enclosed porch area, the security guard was satisfied after viewing her ID via the camera. The doors re-opened automatically, and she approached the desk. The guard re-checked her ID.

'I'm Sergeant Halfpenny and I'll be working for DPR Army,' Mouse said conversationally.

'Hello, love,' he replied, seemingly amused.

Mouse had no idea why he found this funny. 'What's the joke?'

'Well let's just say that most people coming to this building aren't that friendly. I'm Kevin Bassett by the way, but most people call me Bertie. Is that a Welsh accent I detect?'

There was nobody waiting behind Mouse, so they chatted for a few minutes about her background. 'My grandmother was from a village near Cardiff,' said Bertie. 'Mair Bassett. Don't suppose you know her?'

Mouse said she didn't and wondered, not for the first time, why people seemed to think that everyone in Wales knew each other. She was issued her temporary pass, given directions to what would be her new office and told her permanent pass would be ready later that day.

'Some of Simon's staff usually get in around nine o'clock, so if it's ready by then I'll give it to one of them to give to you. Simon runs the central registry and resources room,' he added when he saw the look of confusion on Mouse's face. 'For your department.'

The office was on the ground floor, along one corridor and at the end of another shorter corridor. Luckily for Mouse it wasn't far from the entrance and easy to find. She read the sign on the door – *Brigadier VA Riley, CBE, DPR(A)* – and tried the door saying, 'Shit,' when she discovered it was locked.

'Shit indeed.' Mouse turned at the rather pompous sounding voice. 'And who might you be?' He was dressed in a three-piece pin-striped suit with an old-fashioned gold chain hanging from the pocket on the left side of his waistcoat. The man had an air of authority about him and it was obvious to her that he was somebody important. She resisted the urge to make a smart-arse reply.

'Sergeant Halfpenny, Sir. I'm the new PA until they find a suitable new civvy for Brigadier Riley. Sorry for the language.'

'I see, and where have you come from Sergeant Halfpenny?' He ignored her apology.

'Germany, Sir. And who might you be?'

There was a moment's silence. *I'm in the shit for overstepping the mark,* she thought. But then the man burst out laughing, the sound filling the silent corridor.

'I'm Captain Martin, Sergeant Halfpenny,' he said when he could catch his breath between guffaws. 'And I'm DPR Navy so your boss and I work very closely together. That's Royal Naval Captain by the way. I take it you do know the rank structure of the other services?'

'Yes, Sir, of course.' Mouse was so glad she'd done her homework before taking up her new appointment.

He turned at the sound of footsteps and Mouse did the same. 'Ah, Mr Walker and the lovely Gayle. I take it you're here to show young Sergeant Halfpenny around?' Without waiting for an answer, he turned to Mouse. 'What's your name, Sergeant Halfpenny?'

'Sir?'

Mr Walker smirked and Gayle folded her arms defensively, under her more than ample bust.

'I mean what do your friends call you?'

'Err, Mouse, Sir.'

'Mouse?' he chuckled again. 'Then Mouse it is. Mr Walker here is the warrant officer in charge of you Army personnel here and Gayle is PA to the Chief of the General Staff on the sixth floor. You want to keep away from there, young Mouse,' he whispered the last conspiratorially, 'that's where all the higher-ups work. She's very kindly volunteered to show you the ropes this week.'

'Today, Sir. I'm showing Sergeant Halfpenny the ropes today. I'm far too busy to spend a whole week with her.'

Mr Walker looked down. Mouse wondered if it was to hide his expression from Gayle who she thought, seemed a bit up herself.

'See what I mean about the higher-ups, Mouse,' said Captain Martin. 'And sometimes their staff get delusions of grandeur too.'

Gayle looked furious and Mouse resisted the urge to laugh. They were all in civvies but she knew that the PA to CGS was a warrant officer post so guessed that was Gayle's rank. She had a feeling this woman could make her life difficult if she wanted to, so didn't want to start off their relationship on the wrong foot.

Captain Martin nodded his head to the small group then entered his own office.

'Welcome aboard, Mouse.' Mr Walker held out his hand and she shook it. 'WO1 Pete Walker. My office is in HQ London District, a short walk from this building, and if you need anything, we're your first port of call. Gayle here is the senior female soldier in Main Building but as you can imagine, is very busy.'

'WO2 Johnson,' said Gayle, holding her hand out for Mouse to shake. 'But you can call me ma'am.'

'Yes, Ma'am,' Mouse said, thinking, *at least I know from the off where I stand with you.*

'I'll show you the ropes today but make sure you take notes as I'm far too busy to have to repeat things. Then if you have any issues with the job you can speak to Simon in the registry, or Captain Martin's PA. If you have any other issues and can't get hold of Mr Walker's office, speak to Sergeant Henson in ACGS's office and she'll speak to me if she thinks I need to know.'

'That's Sergeant Cathy Henson,' Mr Walker interjected. 'How's your accommodation and how was your commute this morning?'

They chatted about the Sergeants Mess and her journey to work for a few minutes before WO2 Johnson interrupted.

'Come on then, let's get on,' she said, looking at her watch. 'I don't have time to waste.'

She opened the office and walked in. Mouse followed.

'This is your office and the brigadier's is through there.' Gayle pointed as she talked. The keys to the cupboards and your boss's office are in the safe. The code is 17, 25, 42 and it opens on 75.'

Mouse was trying to take in her new surroundings and to remember the combination. The phone rang and she looked at the warrant officer.

'Well, go on then, answer it.'

'Pen and paper, Ma'am?' She was trying her best not to let the horrible woman intimidate her, but it wasn't easy.

Gayle tutted and picked up the receiver. 'DPR Army's office, Q Johnson speaking,' she said then listened to the voice. 'Yes, Sir that's right. I am and I'm just showing the new temporary PA around. Sergeant Halfpenny, Sir. She's just a stand-in. Not sure but shouldn't be longer than six months, if that.' Mouse watched as *Sir* obviously said something and Gayle giggled flirtatiously.

She left her to it as she approached the combination lock and, facing the wall away from her desk, keyed in the numbers. There was a satisfying click as the door opened the first time and Mouse smiled smugly to herself. She removed the keys and put them on her desk. They had coloured stickers on them, and Mouse noticed the corresponding coloured stickers on the two filing cabinets and a cupboard. She put the key into the cupboard just as *Cow Bag* - as she now thought of Gayle - hung up the phone. Mouse noticed stationery on the third shelf and hastily grabbed a notepad and pen.

'That was Brigadier Harding-Brown, he's coming to visit DPR next Tuesday. You need to tell DPR that he'll arrive by 10 am.'

Mouse quickly wrote down the numbers for the combination, knowing she'd forget them if she didn't. Then she noted the information she'd just been given.

'I thought you'd just passed a shorthand writers' course,' said Q Johnson. 'You'll need to be quicker than that now you're working for a one-star officer.'

Mouse smiled sweetly. 'Thanks for taking that call. What's next then?'

She saw from her expression that she'd wound the warrant officer up and knew she was cutting off her own nose to spite her face. But after the bad business with her husband's murderer and his nasty accomplice, Moira Jones, she was determined not to be bullied or intimidated by anyone in future. She already knew that with old Cow Bag, this would be easier said than done.

'See that green folder in the cupboard?' Cow Bag didn't wait for an answer. 'Well that's the handover notes I've done for you. Have a read of them later and you won't go far wrong.'

'Thanks,' said Mouse thinking that maybe she wasn't such an old Cow Bag after all.

'Right, we've got time for me to orientate you to the building. Come on let's go.'

Mouse locked up as quickly as she could, instinctively knowing she'd be told off if she left things open when the office was empty. *Play the game girl,* she thought as they made their way along the corridor.

She was shown to the departments where she would be expected to run errands for the brigadier or to liaise with other staff. 'And now the most important,' said Cow Bag, as they made their way back towards her office. Gayle veered off along another corridor and into the second room along that path. There were three people in the brew room. A middle-aged man in smart trousers, a shirt, and tie, and two females dressed in skirts, blouses and cardigans. One was older and the other who looked like she'd just left school.

'You can get brews for the boss from here or use the canteen up the escalator on the first floor,' said Gayle.

'And good morning to you, too,' said the man. 'I'm Simon, and you must be the new PA I take it?' Making a point of ignoring Gayle, Simon held his hand out and Mouse shook it, instantly warming to the man. 'This is Felicity,' he pointed to the young woman, 'and May.' They all shook hands and Felicity giggled self-consciously.

'I'm Mouse Halfpenny...'

'That's Sergeant Halfpenny,' Gayle interrupted.

'Nice to meet you, Mouse. Now if Warrant Officer Johnson has no objections, I'll show you around the registry and resources room.'

'I was just about to suggest that. You carry on, Simon, and I'll see you back at your office at 9 o'clock sharp, Sergeant Halfpenny. Don't be late.'

'Yes.... Ma'am.' She added the latter after a suitable pause.

Felicity pulled a face at her back as Cow Bag left and it didn't take much to realise that she wasn't popular with these people either.

The resources room contained the usual fax, and photocopier – both machines looked more modern than those Mouse had used in the past. There were also word processors on a few of the desks in the registry but also some older equipment such as a duplicating machine with the handle on it. With the skin in the machine, the faster the handle was cranked, the more copies could be produced. It could be tiring on the arm and hand and Mouse couldn't imagine the waiflike Felicity using it for very long.

'You support your brigadier,' said Simon, 'and we support the officers and Civil Servants in the department who don't have their own PAs, and also help you guys with any big distribution or despatch jobs, if required.'

He gave a brief explanation of the roles of the other staff, two of whom Mouse hadn't yet met. They didn't look up from their desks as Simon spoke, so she didn't introduce herself or attempt to shake hands. *Some people can be bloody rude,* she thought, knowing that this place was totally different to every other unit she'd served at. Even though there had been lots of civvies in the headquarters in Rheindahlen, there was a different vibe here and despite it being the first day, Mouse had already noticed there certainly wasn't a feeling of all being in it together like there had been in Germany, even though she hadn't got on with everyone there. Military staff wore civvies too, so Mouse had to have her wits about her to ensure she gave the proper level of respect to those who deserved it. It didn't occur to her that most people she passed while going about her daily duties would probably think she was a civilian.

'I don't want to bamboozle you on your first day,' said Simon, 'so as soon as Les gets in, we'll get you issued with your new travel card.' Mouse looked confused. 'You have to go on errands outside the building as well as inside, sometimes to areas outside zone one and Mill Hill is what, zone four?'

Mouse nodded.

'You may have to go as far as zone six to collect or deliver packages or other information, and you'll need an all areas, all zones travel card. Les is the travel clerk. Try not to take any notice of the way he looks at you, he can be a bit, err...'

'He's a flaming pervert, Mouse,' said May. 'And I would advise you only to speak to him when others are present and then only when you have to.'

Felicity seemed to become agitated so May got up and walked the short distance to her. 'It's all right, love, he can't hurt you.'

'What the...?'

'He is different,' Simon defended the man Mouse hadn't yet met. 'But he's a good worker and rest assured, if I thought he meant any harm to anyone in this department, I'd have him thrown out quicker than you could say....'

One of the men working at his desk who hadn't acknowledged Mouse started coughing uncontrollably. May was the first to get to him and gave him a sharp thump on the back. Simon joined them quickly followed by Felicity.

As Mouse watched she felt, rather than heard, a presence behind her. Turning, she tried to hide her surprise when the man looking directly at her was the same man who had leered at her on the underground train, earlier that morning. He smirked as he looked down and she felt the others looking at her.

'I take it you're Les?' she said, and he looked up then nodded and folded his arms at the same time. 'I'm Sergeant Halfpenny,' she said. 'Simon said you're going to issue me a new travelcard?'

'Umm, yeah, that's right. Give me a chance, love.'

'It's Sergeant Halfpenny, or Mouse, but never love. I'll give you a chance to get sorted and I'll come back in ten minutes for my card.'

'But you're not my...'

'Make sure it's ready by the time I come back. And I suggest you watch your manners when travelling on public transport, if you don't want to be reported to the police.' She turned to Simon. 'Thanks for the guided tour, I'm looking forward to working with you all.'

Mouse left without further ado, smiling to herself at the look of surprise on Les's face; he clearly didn't like being told what to do by women and wasn't used to people being so straight with him. She must have made the others wonder what had happened on her way into work, though she suspected they had more than a good idea. Yes, to call Les a horse's arse was an insult to horses. She knew she was going to enjoy winding him up at every available opportunity.

Her smile soon vanished when she found Cow Bag outside her office waiting for her. 'You're late Sergeant Halfpenny.' Mouse didn't bother checking her watch. 'Sorry, Ma'am, got held up waiting for the guy who issues the travel cards. I have to go back later when it's ready.'

'I don't want to hear your excuses,' she said as they entered the office. 'The brigadier will be in soon, he likes his coffee NATO standard, preferably with a bar of chocolate I'm told.'

'Okay, I'll go and put the kettle on then.'

'You do that. I have an emergency to attend to upstairs. All the phone numbers you need are in the notes I've written. Sergeant Henson is your first point of contact if you need anything that the registry staff can't handle, but I will, of course, deal with any emergencies beyond your or her capabilities.'

'Thanks, Ma'am, that's good to know.' Mouse was straight-faced and could see Cow Bag trying to work out whether she was taking the mickey. Thankfully, she decided not to make anything of the comment.

Cow Bag put both hands on the lapels of her tailored jacket and gave them a lift before speaking. 'Try not to bother me and keep out of trouble.'

As she watched her walk along the corridor Mouse wondered how the rest of the British Army had managed while Warrant Officer Class 2 Johnson had been showing her the ropes. She also wondered how she managed to walk with that big pole stuck up her fat backside. *Why can't people just be bloody nice to each other*, she thought, as she filled the kettle in the kitchen and prepped the coffee for the new boss. Hopefully he would be a good egg. If what she'd heard was true, he sounded a bit like a genius nutty professor with a brain the size of an elephant.

Back in the office, Mouse was reading her notes and working out what button did what on the new-fangled word processor. Lost in concentration, she almost jumped when she heard the voice. 'How about ya, you must be my new PA.' The words were followed by a hearty chuckle which made her smile.

'Yes, Sir,' she said rising to her feet. 'Sergeant Halfpenny.'

The brigadier held out his hand. 'Pleased to meet you.' The shake was very vigorous and for such a small man he had an extremely tight and strong grip. 'Sergeant Halfpenny, eh?'

'Yes, Sir.'

'Well, welcome on board, Sergeant Halfpenny. What's your first name?'

'I'm known as Mouse, Sir.'

'So that's what it is then. And I bet that your grumpy old warrant officer won't be amused at that, eh, Mouse.' He chuckled loudly as he made his way into his office and she followed. Nobody had told her that her new boss was so charismatic and witty, and she liked him already.

'Coffee, Mouse, I take it...'

'Milk and two sugars, Sir, just be a minute.'

'That's what I like to hear. Don't suppose you've got a Kit Kat?'

'Not yet, Sir, but I can soon remedy that.'

Less than five minutes later Mouse took in the coffee and Kit Kat she'd hurriedly purchased from the snack bar on the first floor.

'Thank you,' the boss said sincerely. 'Grab your own coffee and a notepad and I'll let you know this week's schedule.'

She did as instructed.

'Now, Monday is meeting day where we catch up from the Press Office on what's happened during the weekend, and what's been in the media. I won't have time to talk to you properly today, perhaps not for the rest of the week either. But if you think there's anything urgent work-wise, make sure I'm the first, not last to know. Got it?'

'Yes, Sir.'

'And you know who to go to for help if you need it?'

'Sergeant Henson, Sir, then Mr Walker or Q Johnson as a last resort.'

'Good. But Simon will help you if you need it, or May or that young niece of hers.'

'Yes, Sir.'

'Now down to business. Have you got three quid?'

'Um, I think I should have, Sir.'

'Excellent. Can you lend it to me?'

'Yes, Sir, I'll just...'

'What I need you to do, Mouse is to go to Embankment Station and ask for Mike Partridge at the ticket office. Give him two pounds eighty and tell him Paddy Riley is as good as his word.'

Seeing the look of confusion on her face he elaborated. 'I forgot my wallet and managed to get onto the underground without a ticket, it wasn't so easy coming out at Embankment.'

'Okay, Sir, what about your return journey and your needs through the day.'

He opened his desk drawer and produced a bank card. 'I'll go to the bank later, but thanks for the offer,' he said. 'Close the door on your way out.'

Suitably dismissed, Mouse left the office wondering how some of these officers managed to command so many soldiers when they seemed to struggle with day-to-day basics. He did have a sharp brain so she assumed the brigadier could tell her the cubic capacity of a bottle but would probably ask her to open it for him. Still, she had a legitimate reason for a stroll through parts of central London. She intended to get her new travel card from Les the perv, and then make her way to Embankment to see Mike Partridge.

The brigadier left the office just after six that evening, and Mouse wasn't far behind him. By the time she reached the Sergeants Mess it was well after seven and the dining room was like a scene from the old TV show *Survivors*. Scrub that, thought Mouse, nobody was about, not even ten percent of the population. She opened the large fridge and found three plated meals in there. The one with her name on it was covered in cling film like the others and contained a pasty looking piece of quiche with some limp lettuce, sad looking tomatoes and cucumber, and a chopped boiled egg where the white had started to turn grey. She removed the cling film and took a bite of the quiche. As hungry as she was Mouse couldn't stomach it and made her way to her room, thankful that she had some snacks in one of the cupboards. She made herself a cup of tea and chomped on the crisps and chocolate as she watched an old episode of Day of the Triffids. Even though the job was going to be interesting, Mouse knew she couldn't live like this for six months and planned on spending as little time as possible in this Mess.

Cathy Henson called in to see her the following day. 'Sorry I didn't get down to see you yesterday,' she said. 'It was a bloody nightmare day upstairs.' She didn't elaborate. 'Did Q give you my handover notes?'

'Your handover notes? She said she'd done them for me?'

'Taken the credit for that as well has she? Why doesn't that surprise me?'

Mouse shook her head. She liked Cathy Henson already.

'At least you don't have to work with the old bag,' said Cathy and they both laughed. 'Listen, some of us go out on Thursday nights as most people bomb blast as soon as they finish work on Friday and you won't see them again until work on Monday, and that's only if you work in the same area. It can be quite isolating here, not like a proper unit, and we have to look out for each other.'

That was the best news Mouse had heard since starting work. 'Sounds good to me, Cathy. What's the plan?'

'We're going to Wong Kei's in Soho for some scoff this week. Then we'll find a bar for few drinks. I'll give you a shout at six. If your boss plans on working after that, you may have to catch up with us there, but arrange his diary so he leaves earlier on future Thursdays.'

'Got it. But how the hell am I supposed to find my way around Soho if he does decide to work late?'

'Well from what I've heard, you can be quite resourceful,' Cathy gave a knowing smile. 'See you on Thursday if I don't see you before, and,' she listened for a second to make sure nobody else was about, 'don't let the old bag wind you up. The more she thinks she upsets you the nastier she is. If you're not bothered, she'll soon get bored and move onto someone else.'

'She must be really unhappy if that's how she gets her kicks.'

'Dunno and don't care either. I just hope that karma comes and bites her in the bum one day, and that I'm around to see it.'

Mouse knew life was too short to let the likes of Q Johnson spoil it, but sometimes it was hard not to.

'See you Thursday, Cathy, and thanks.'

'Anytime, Mouse.'

*****

Each day was busier than the previous, but Mouse relished being busy, especially dealing with the unusual requests from the brigadier. She accepted that she'd have to run the usual errands required of a PA, such as making sure he had enough refreshments and lunch when he was working, but she also did shopping at his request, visited the dry cleaners and even went out for cards or gifts for birthdays or anniversaries of his relatives. His family lived in their own home in Northern Ireland and the brigadier was accommodated in a small flat in central London. This was the arrangement for a number of the senior officers, and they seemed happy enough to work long hours during the week, leave early on a Friday, and start late on a Monday, if their duties allowed. It was often a different story for the Director of Public Relations when incidents during the weekend had to be dealt with on a Monday morning, which involved contact with, and mass statements to, the media. The MOD Press Office was manned all day every day and the DPRs of each service were called on Sunday evenings if there was anything they had to deal with as a matter of urgency on a Monday. Mouse discovered that nothing had kicked off on the Sunday prior to her starting the job which made her first Monday relatively quiet for the brigadier, compared to those he usually called *Holy Hell!*

Thursday came around pretty quickly and Mouse didn't know whether she was coming or going. Members of the British Forces had shot suspected terrorists in Gibraltar. The phones were ringing off the hook, and the whole department, as well as the rest of the MOD was buzzing. DPR had been called to the office of the man who headed up the Army, Chief of the General Staff, along with Director Special Forces. He hadn't returned by the time Cathy appeared at the office, thirty minutes later than arranged.

'I suppose it's a stupid question to ask whether you're ready to come out to play?'

'Yup. Boss is still with CGS, no idea what time he'll be back.'

'Okay. Well we're still going for some scoff and a quick drink. God knows we all need a drink after a day like today,' she added putting her hands on her head and shaking it dramatically.

'It's not the first time the IRA have fucked up my social life and I'm sure it won't be the last.' Mouse answered and Cathy laughed.

'Do you want to meet us there later or will you go straight back to the Mess?'

'I'll need something to eat,' said Mouse, 'but from what I hear it's in the middle of Soho and not an easy place to find.'

'It's not that difficult.' Cathy started to reel off the directions, unaware that Mouse's directional compass was totally skew-whiff. Not wishing to look a complete numpty, Mouse nodded and made affirmative sounds, but after 'the next right after the ice-cream parlour,' she had totally lost interest and decided she'd have Chinese for tea anyway, whether or not she made it to Wong Kei's

'Get that?'

'Think so.'

'I'm impressed. See you there later then?'

'Depends, Cathy. If it's too late, I'll grab a quick something on the way to the tube and will catch up with you tomorrow.'

'I'm off home tomorrow. Long weekend. In fact, Mouse, why don't you come down when you finish tomorrow night, or even on Saturday. We have one of those put-you-up beds. It'll be a tight squeeze in my room but it'll fit.'

'I'm not sure, Cathy...'

'No worries if you've got other plans.'

She didn't and the thought of staying in the Mess on her own during the weekend wasn't at all appealing.

'I haven't and I'd love to, thank you. Tomorrow's going to be another busy day so how about I come on Saturday, stay overnight and come back on Sunday.'

They made the arrangements and Mouse tried not to look too surprised when Cathy gave her the address. She didn't tell her she'd visited that area before, in what Mouse now thought of as her previous life.

The brigadier arrived just after Cathy left, so Mouse didn't have time to dwell on their conversation.

'How about ya, Mouse. Any messages?'

'Loads, Sir, all on your desk but the most important is from the Editor of The Sun. You may want to call him first.'

'Shit. Okay, will do. There's no more you can do for me today, so get me a brew then get yourself off. I'm meeting with DSF tomorrow so early start tomorrow. I need you in for seven o'clock.'

'Yes, Sir,' she said before getting up to go to the kitchen.

'Anything for eating?' asked the boss.

'There's a tuna and cucumber sandwich in the fridge, Sir. Shall I bring it in with your coffee?'

'Please. Anything else?'

'Read the note on your desk, Sir,' she called with a smile as she left the office. By the time Mouse returned with the coffee the brigadier had found the note telling him to look in his top drawer and he'd already consumed the Twix bar. There was still a Kit Kat and a Bounty left but Mouse knew she'd need to do a replen the following day. As much as her boss liked the new editor of the country's favourite red-top newspaper, she knew he needed all the chocolate he could get his hands on after a call with the man.

'Goodnight, Sir. Don't work too late.'

'I wish.' Then, to her surprise, he added, 'You're good at this, Mouse. You should consider it as a long-term career.'

'Thanks, Sir. I will.' The brigadier was a decent sort but wasn't one for giving compliments, so Mouse was walking on air as she left work. Until she started thinking about how proud Guy would be of her. It took the shine off her mood and the loneliness hit again, like someone had thrust a dagger into her heart and twisted it. She stopped for a second to catch her breath. That was the trouble with grief, you never knew when or where it could hit you. Recomposing herself, she left the building and made her way towards Soho. She couldn't face the thought of returning to her room, even for a few hours before trying to sleep, and she needed to be around people, even if they were anonymous strangers. To take her mind off Guy, Mouse decided to try to find the Chinese restaurant in Soho, knowing before she started that she was likely to fail miserably.

She was proper chuffed with herself having managed to find her way to the ice cream parlour Cathy had talked about when giving her the directions. Knowing she had a crap sense of direction should have stopped her there, but this gave her something different to think about other than basking in self-pity, so she continued. A few minutes later she lost her way so decided to head back to the ice cream parlour and get some food from the deli next door. It didn't take much longer to realise she was totally lost and had no idea which direction the ice cream parlour was. *All is not lost!* She chuckled to herself at that thought and a few passersby gave her a wide berth. Looking around at the shops, restaurants and people, she guessed she was either in Soho or Chinatown but was unsure of which as she didn't know the area. Her plan was to continue walking until she found an underground station. She could easily navigate the clever underground map and would soon find her way home to the Mess. Her stomach rumbled and she decided to stop for food sooner rather than later. Turning down one of the narrow streets, Mouse stopped to look at the menu in the window of a Chinese looking restaurant. They had both Chicken Chow Mein and Szechuan Pork on the menu, two of her favourites, so she looked to see how busy the restaurant was – always a good guide to the quality of food. To say she was surprised at who she saw sitting in the restaurant was an understatement. Q Johnson was smiling at a man sitting opposite. He looked older and had an air of authority that she could spot even from outside. As she watched, they reached their hands out to each other. The man picked up her hand and caressed it with his lips – it was far too long to be just a kiss and was plainly obvious that they were more than friends.

'Well, I'll go to our house,' Mouse said out loud as she considered whether to brazen it out and go into the restaurant to eat. Deciding she couldn't actually face Cow Bag after such a stressful day in the office, she decided to find somewhere else. She continued walking and eventually found herself at Leicester Square. Mouse had a hurried meal in McDonalds then made her way back to the Sergeants Mess in Mill Hill. She couldn't wait to see Cathy on Saturday to tell her who she'd seen. They both thought Q was too up her own arse to have a boyfriend and the thought of her *doing it* with someone was like imagining pensioners at it. Yuck! Saying that, knowing what a nasty woman Cow Bag could be, it might be useful ammunition to have if she ever wanted to wind her up. Perhaps she should keep this one to herself for now.

Mouse got off the underground at Melham station and made her way along the corridor, up the first set of escalators and along another corridor and escalator before exiting through a turnstile. Being a Saturday it wasn't as busy as it would have been at rush hours during the week, but some people were still in *London mode* as she liked to think of it. Rushing about their business like busy little ants, heads down and pretty much ignoring what was going on all around them.

She looked around as she left the station. Nothing was familiar as the last time she'd visited had been by car. She'd gone from crematorium to car, to pub, back to car, then home with Elaine, so hadn't seen much of the area on that occasion. Elaine was now living in York and if she saw Jill's mother or sister, they visited her.

Mouse followed the signs out of the station for *Melham Market*, Cathy having told her to head in that direction and she would meet her outside the ornate green arch, which was the market entrance. It was less than a ten-minute walk, then another ten minutes waiting for her friend to arrive.

'Hello, butty,' said a voice behind her and Mouse laughed at Cathy's pathetic attempt at a Welsh accent. 'You found it all right then?'

The girls greeted each other. 'Ready for some scoff?' asked Cathy.

Mouse hadn't realised how hungry she was, but Cathy's comment reminded her. 'I'm starving actually. Shall we eat then do some sightseeing?'

'It's bloody Melham, Mouse not central London. There ain't much to see here except the people. Mix of wannabe Yuppies and a bunch of gangsters who are most likely a lot richer than the wannabies. We can have a look round the market and shops later if you like? Come on.' Cathy linked her arm into Mouse's and they walked to the end of the High Street. She didn't give Mouse a chance to get a word in as she chattered about her family and upbringing. Being on her home turf had certainly made the words flow and Mouse hadn't heard Cathy talk so much. She looked around while she listened to Cathy. Some of the properties were shops with what looked like flats above them, and others were small houses. The area was buzzing as people went about their business.

'So basically I thought me mum and dad were me older brother and sister.'

'Jesus! What happened when you found out and how old were you? It must have been awful.'

'Understatement, Mouse. Me dad was killed in a motorbike accident when he was just twenty-two and I was eight years old. Me gran, who I thought was me mum, got pissed at the funeral and told me everything. So I lost my father and gained a mother and a grandmother all in the same day.'

'Oh, Cathy, poor you. That must have been a dreadful shock.' Mouse went to put her arms around her friend, but Cathy put her hands up to stop her.

'It's okay, Mouse. That was then and this is now. Yeah it was bloody awful at the time and I went off the rails for a while. But I'm over it now. Me gran died a few years back and there's just me and me mum now, and a few distant cousins. She's done everything she can for me. Worked her socks off and gone without a lot so I could have holidays and nice birthday and Christmas presents. She made a mistake when her and me dad were kids, but she's made up for it since and I just want her to be happy.'

They turned a corner and Mouse did a double-take when she saw the sign for *The Carpenters*. The memories of Jill's wake came flooding back as if it were yesterday, not more than two years before. And the conversation about Cathy's family stopped abruptly.

'You all right, Mouse? Looks like you've seen a ghost.'

'I'm fine. Guess I've gone too long without eating and I just felt a bit dizzy, that's all.'

'We'll soon sort that. They do great food in The Carps. It used to be a hang-out for all the bad 'uns but it's had a makeover and gone upmarket, and so have the gangsters, ha ha.' Cathy laughed at her own joke.

'Gangsters?' Mouse asked, wondering how much to tell her new friend.

'Yeah. I know all about your mate who died, Mouse, so you don't have to pretend.'

'You knew Jill and her family?'

'Everyone round here knows Jill's family. They might be on the wrong side of the law but if you leave them alone and mind your own business, they don't bother you. And some of them even look after those less fortunate shall we say.'

'I see. Did you know Jill?'

'Nah. Me mum's a hairdresser so hears pretty much all the gossip. When someone told her about a Welsh girl who was in the Army with Jill and who'd lost her husband,' she shrugged her shoulders. 'Well it didn't take the brains of an Archbishop to work it all out, Mouse.'

'Fair enough. Shall we go in?'

Mouse almost fell as she went to push open the door. The person holding it looked as gobsmacked as she did.

'Well, if it ain't the young Welshie soldier and soldier Cathy too. Come on in girls and I'll buy you a drink.'

He was instantly recognisable due to the scar down one side of his face and his iffy eye. But even if she hadn't seen him, there was no mistaking that Soprano sounding voice.

'I'll see you next month, mate,' Earl said to a departing man as he walked out of the door. Mouse was distracted as the man was the biggest Chinese man she had ever seen. Even though he was dressed in a suit, she could tell he was very muscly. 'You certainly will, my friend,' the man replied in heavily accented English.

The girls followed Earl to the bar and he took their orders. 'Vodka eh, Welshie. Very sophisticated. Come on, let's get a booth.'

They made themselves comfortable and Mouse looked around, noting that the place had received a makeover since her one and only previous visit. The leather seats in the booths had been reupholstered and the bar's deco was minimalist but stylish.

'It looks really nice in here now,' she said. 'Proper stylish.'

'Thanks,' Earl replied. 'They took my advice and went for the monochrome look. Minimalistic but stylish and effective don't you think?'

Mouse laughed. 'Pull the other one,' she said until she realised he wasn't kidding. 'Oh, I'm sorry, I...'

'She didn't mean anything by it.' Cathy interrupted.

Earl laughed. 'I know I don't exactly look like an interior designer, but I'm a man of many talents and that's one of them.'

'It's well nice,' said Mouse and Earl raised an eyebrow. 'No really, I mean it. You could probably do this for a living.'

It was his turn to laugh now. 'Let's not get too carried away, love, eh. Do you girls like steak?' He asked, changing the subject. 'Because this place does the best steak and chips in the whole of London.'

'Sounds lovely,' Cathy replied, and Mouse nodded her agreement.

'Right, Cathy. Go and order the food for the three of us and ask Larry for a bottle of their best champagne. Don't hurry back.'

Cathy got the message but wasn't happy as she wondered what Big Earl wanted to discuss with Mouse. 'Go on then, love, chop-chop.'

'How are you doing?' the big man asked as soon as Cathy was out of earshot.

Mouse ignored the question. 'Thanks for dealing with KC and sending us the photos. It meant a lot to me and Elaine.'

'Don't know what you mean, love,' he said, grinning. 'I trust you haven't discussed that issue?'

'Of course not, and I never will either.' She drew a line across her mouth as if zipping it closed.

'Good. Now, how are you? I know it's been a few years but that means nothing sometimes.' She had no idea how he knew how she felt.

Mouse felt the tears threaten and was annoyed. She was having a conversation with a gangster for God's sake, but the big man definitely had a soft side to him and seemed genuinely concerned.

'It's the worst thing that will ever happen to you, love,' he said as he put a hand on her lower arm. 'And trust me, you will learn to live again without feeling guilty, perhaps you'll even find someone else to make you happy.'

'I very much doubt that,' said Mouse.

'I'm sure he wouldn't want you to waste your life, Mouse.'

'How do you know what he'd want?' she asked, raising her voice so some of the other customers looked their way. One look from Earl told them to mind their own business and they lowered their eyes or carried on with their own conversations.

'Because if it was me, that's what I'd want and if he loved you as much as you loved him, he'd want you to live your life and to be happy.'

Seeing Earl had brought the memories flooding back and his thoughtfulness also struck a nerve. This time the tears came and Cathy and the bar manager watched as Earl comforted her friend. It seemed odd to her that a man who was capable of immense cruelty, was also capable of such kindness and compassion.

When Mouse was all cried out she lifted her head, embarrassed. 'Sorry about that. Sometimes it just happens.'

'No need to be sorry, love. Life can be pretty shit at times and you just have to get through it.' He paused to let the words sink in. 'Right then. I'll check on the food and drinks while you go and wash your face.' Mouse got up straight away and did exactly as he'd suggested.

Despite the fact that he was a gangster, he was good company and they enjoyed themselves. The meal finished Earl was about to order a second bottle of bubbly when Mouse put up her hand.

'I haven't met Cathy's mam yet and don't want to be pissed before I even get there. I think we'd better make a move, Cathy.' She felt tiddly already and didn't want to give the wrong first impression. It was a sobering thought as up until a few hours ago she wouldn't have given a toss.

'Maeve's a good girl,' said Earl. 'And she won't mind at all.' Seeing the look on Mouse's face he added, 'but you have to do what you have to do. Why don't you have a coffee before you go? That'll make you feel better.' There was something about Mouse that brought out his protective instinct and he also didn't want to see her unhappy either. He guessed he was at least ten years older than her and wondered about the strength of his feelings. Something had been there at Jill's funeral, but he'd assumed that was the emotion of the occasion and, knowing she had a husband had been able to suppress any urges. But now? He let his thoughts wander.

The silence brought him back to the present and he looked at the girls who were both staring at him, then they looked at each other.

'Mouse said she'd love a coffee thanks, Earl and me too.'

'Go on then, Cathy.'

Cathy sighed loudly as she stood up and walked slowly to the bar, like a teenager being told to tidy her bedroom. Mouse chuckled to herself and Earl smiled. 'Don't worry,' he said, 'me and Maeve are like that...' He squeezed two fingers together. 'Cathy's used to me telling her what to do.'

'So you and Cathy's mum are together?'

'We haven't made it public, love, but it's looking that way. But it doesn't have to be. I can wait if...'

Mouse wondered what he meant by the last bit. The only feelings she had for him were akin to the affection like he was a kind uncle type figure. And anyway, as kind as he could be, he was too far on the wrong side of the law and she knew he could also be extremely cruel.

'Even though I don't know her yet, I'm sure you'll be very happy together.'

They drank their coffees and chatted amiably until Earl decided it was time for him to leave. 'Bye, you two. Cathy, tell your mum I'll pick her up at 7 o'clock tonight and to wear something dressy.' Mouse noticed the look of surprise on Cathy's face and made a mental note to speak to her about it later.

'I'll just use the loo before we go,' Cathy said. 'Thanks for treating us, Earl.'

He waited until Cathy was well on the way to the ladies before speaking again. 'It was great to see you, Welshie.'

'It was nice to see you again too, Earl, and thanks for the meal. That was very generous of you.'

Earl engulfed her in a bear hug and Mouse was surprised to find she enjoyed the feel of his arms around her.

'Bye, Welshie. Until we meet again.'

It was a strange thing to say as she had no intention of meeting up with him again.

'You didn't know about Earl and your mother?' she asked Cathy as soon as they were on their own. 'Damn right I didn't, and I'll tell you something else too, my mother doesn't know about it either, so that'll be interesting.' She winked at Mouse and linked her arm into her friend's again, while Mouse wondered why Cathy's mother hadn't told her daughter she'd been seeing Earl.

'Come on, let's get out of here and you can tell me why Melham's favourite gangster wanted to speak to you in private.'

Mouse sighed. 'It was just about Jill and her family and we talked about Guy. It brought it all back like it was yesterday and you could see how upset I was.'

'Whatever you say, Mouse. Let's go and check out the shops.'

*****

They arrived at Cathy's a few hours later, laden with bags of new clothes – mostly from the market – and the fruit and veg that Cathy's mum had told her to buy. The woman who opened the door wasn't how Mouse had mentally pictured her. Maeve looked more like Cathy's older sister than her mother. She was stunning with a lovely figure and glossy long black hair that was tied back in a ponytail, with a few wisps framing her oval face. She had kind brown eyes, which were almond shaped and like pools of liquid chocolate. Yes, Cathy's mum was definitely one of the most beautiful looking people Mouse had ever set eyes on, and on first impressions, she acted as if she didn't know how gorgeous she really was.

'Hello, my love, so you're Cathy's new friend. I've heard all about you, you know. Not only from Cathy but you're known to the Cartwright's too. They're not as bad as everyone makes out you know. Look after their own they do, and only mess with those who deserve it. In fact...'

'Mum! Give Mouse a chance to get a word in for Pete's sake!'

'I'm sorry, love. I do go on at times. It's coz I'm a hairdresser and people expect it. In fact I was just saying to one of the old biddies the other day...'

'Mum!'

'Nice to meet you, Mrs...' Mouse said.

'You can call me Maeve, lovey. We don't stand on ceremony round here. Where have you girls been anyway, I expected you earlier?'

'We had lunch in the Carps, Mum. Big Earl treated us.'

37

'Oh he did, did he? And what did he have to say for himself?'

'Well actually, he said he'd pick you up at 7 o'clock tonight and to wear something dressy. Honestly.' She added the last after seeing the look on her mother's face.

'Oh my Lord!' That only gives me four hours and I haven't got anything decent to wear. I've only been out with him casually before like. I'll have to get my rollers in and put a face pack on and do me nails. And when will I have the time to go out and buy something. Lordy, Lord. Why didn't he give me some notice? How the hell am I supposed to be ready in time? What am I going to do, Cathy?' She looked really worried which made Mouse realise how keen she must be on Earl.

'What do you mean casually? So you've been on dates with him before?' asked Cathy.

'I wouldn't call them dates, love. We've had a few drinks in the Carps, gone to watch the dogs once and I even stood in the cold with him one afternoon to watch the football. Jeans and jumper stuff so I didn't even dress up! But this sounds like a proper date, so he's noticed me at last. Oh gawd!'

Cathy was beginning to appreciate that her mother had her own life while she was getting on with her own Army career. She wanted to know more but didn't want to add to her mother's agitation. Her questions would keep for another time. It's okay, Mum. Shall we go through your wardrobe and find you something nice to wear?'

'But I don't have anything.'

'What about that black dress with the silver bits on the padded shoulders? That's dead fashionable, Mum, all the models are wearing padded shoulders and it looks great on you with your small waist too.'

'Ooh, I forgot about that. You girls go and have a look then and I'll get cracking. I've been waiting ages for this to happen and I don't want to mess it up.'

*****

Back in the Sergeants' Mess on Sunday evening, Mouse was getting her kit ready for the following week and reflecting on what had happened in Melham. They'd thought Cathy's mum was in bed sleeping when they returned from the club during the early hours of the morning, but she still hadn't made an appearance when Cathy was making a bacon butty that morning and turned up just before Mouse left at midday.

Maeve was singing to herself and cracking jokes and it was obvious to them both that she'd had a great night.

'Bye, love. Nice to meet you and hope to see you again,' she said, before adding that she was going for a kip as she hadn't had much sleep the night before.

'Aw, Mum, for Pete's sake. I don't wanna hear that.' Cathy had put her hands to her ears and started singing. Her mother laughed, they said their final goodbyes to Mouse and that's how she left them.

Although it had been good fun, when she was ironing her trousers, skirts and blouses, Mouse reminded herself that she had to find a way out of London, preferably to a job in Hong Kong where she would have the company of her brother's family during her down time. Wondering how she could achieve this, she didn't know that an opportunity would present itself in the form of a visiting brigadier, during the following week.

Chapter 3 – Planning for a Posting

Back at work on Monday morning, Mouse was in business-like mode as she looked through the diary. Monday mornings were always manic with the fallout from the weekend dramas. Although the boss was pretty affable, events during the weekend could cause severe stress and his mood could swing from good to bad at the flick of a switch. She'd read the press reports already and it had been a slow weekend for the military, with no major incidents. Because there weren't many newsworthy military happenings, a few *'drunken squaddie'* stories had hit the press, and one of an officer taking photos of himself in unusual clothes. Mouse chuckled as she looked at the photo again of the stupid man in mess kit from neck to waist, then stockings, suspenders and stiletto heels. The photo next to him was of his wife who was dressed in a beige twinset and brown plaid skirt. *Who knew what went on behind closed doors?* She chuckled again and wondered if his wife joined in with him or if it was his dirty little secret.

She heard voices along the corridor and looked up.

'How about you, Mouse?'

She folded up the paper and stood up. 'Good morning, Sir. How are you today?'

Although he'd told her not to stand on ceremony, Mouse always stood up to greet her boss the first time she saw him each week. Whether or not she liked or disliked certain officers didn't matter a jot. The fact that they had earned the Queen's Commission meant she would give their rank the respect it deserved, even if she thought the person underneath the uniform was a complete tosser. Thankfully her boss was a good man, so she didn't mind, but she didn't know how she felt about the man who was standing next to him and looking at her as the brigadier spoke. Mouse recognised him as Q Johnson's dinner date from the previous Thursday. 'This is my old pal Brigadier Harding-Brown, Mouse, we went through Sandhurst together all those years ago.'

'Pleased to meet you, Sir,' she said, and shook the hand that he held out. He held onto hers a touch too long. She had him down to visit the following day, but it would be no trouble to make extra coffee and to pop up to the shop to get some biscuits as required.

'Miles is a day early, Mouse. He's with CGS before me but we've time for coffee before that.' You've seen it then, I take it?' he added, nodding towards the newspaper she had been scanning.

'I certainly have, Sir,' she responded, knowing he was talking about *mess kit gate* as she thought of it.

'Why do we employ these idiots, eh, Mouse?'

'Is that a rhetorical question, Sir? She looked from one brigadier to the other and they both laughed.

'I'll get your coffees, Sir, and is it too early for chocolate?'

'It's never too early for chocolate. Bring the goodies in with our coffees, quick as you can.'

Mouse excused herself and headed for the kitchen. Waiting for the kettle to boil she wondered about Q and the visiting brigadier. It was unlikely that he was single so, if he wasn't, it meant that they were having an affair which his wife probably didn't know about. If he was, the Army was old-fashioned in her eyes and would frown on a relationship between a warrant officer and senior officer - standards had to be maintained after all. She hurried back to the office, as fast as she could without risking spilling any of the coffee, took two Kit Kat bars out of the drawer, put them on the tray and took it into her boss's office.

'So you think there's a connection between the Chinese man they found dead in Germany and the 14K Triads? Are they... Ah, here's the coffee, Miles.' Brigadier Riley changed conversation as Mouse walked into the office, but she'd heard enough to have an idea of what they were talking about.

Brigadier Riley picked up his Kit Kat from the tray and opened it as Mouse set the tray on the table. 'Thanks, Mouse,' he said, in between taking a bite out of the chocolate.

'Pleasure, Sir,' she replied, then added conversationally, 'I found the body of Chinese Pete in the

Sergeants Mess in JHQ. They thought there was a Triad connection, Sir.'

Brigadier Riley spluttered pieces of chocolate and biscuit over the table and Brigadier Harding-Brown chuckled before saying. 'So you're aware they are predominantly Chinese organised crime groups? The 14K headquarters is in Hong Kong but they operate throughout the world.'

'And you think the man I found in Germany is connected to this group, Sir and that his murder…?'

'Thanks for the coffee, Sergeant Halfpenny,' Brigadier Riley said. 'Close the door on your way out.'

'Yes, Sir.' Mouse knew she had overstepped the mark but knew her boss well enough to know he wouldn't bollock her if she stopped there. She left the office wondering even more about Hong Kong. Having just met the current Deputy Commander of British Forces Hong Kong if her suspicions were correct, he had the morals of an alley cat. She planned on working that to her advantage but would need further evidence to ensure she wasn't barking up the wrong tree.

Later in the week any plans of her own were put to the back of her mind as the dreadful news came in that two soldiers had been viciously murdered in Northern Ireland on one day – one nil to the IRA – then a few days later three suspected IRA terrorists had been shot dead on a Mediterranean island – one to the good guys.

The brigadier was in early on Thursday and asked her to book a table at the Ivy for him and Brigadier Harding-Brown who was still in town.

'Get a brew and come into the office. I've more tasks for you.'

They'll no doubt involve collecting his dry-cleaning or some such chore she thought as she made her way to the kitchen.

Ten minutes later, Mouse was sitting at the table in the brigadier's office taking notes, as he sat at his desk chomping loudly on his Mars bar.

'So, I'll finish this report then you can take it to Q Johnson. CGS wants to see me at eleven hundred hours so it will give him plenty of time to read it. While I'm in with the general, pop down to the jewellers and pick up that nice gold necklace for Mrs Riley. I've paid a deposit so here's the receipt and the sixty quid I owe them. Can you get her a card from me too, Mouse? One of those padded jobs with 'beautiful wife' or 'love of my life'? She loves the soppy stuff, so that'll put me in her good books. Then I'll have a tuna and cucumber sandwich on brown from the deli for when I get back at one-ish, and a Kit Kat to see me through the afternoon.'

Mouse continued to take note of the other jobs he wanted done during the rest of the day when he was going to be out. As she left his office she was chuffed she had a reason to go to see Cow Bag and planned on speaking to her about her dinner date with Brigadier Harding-Brown.

'That's it,' the boss said. 'Except that Brigadier Harding-Brown has other plans for the weekend so I'll be off home after dinner tonight to spend Mrs Riley's birthday with her. You can take tomorrow off, too, if you get this lot done.'

'Thanks, Sir. That'll be great.'

She decided she wouldn't speak to Cow Bag just yet and wondered if she'd have anything more juicy to discuss with her or her brigadier, come Monday morning.

Up in CGS's outer office on the sixth floor of the ministry, Mouse decided to have some fun.

'Hiya, Q. How are you today?'

Cow Bag almost gave her thoughts away but managed to eventually mask her surprise at the friendly question from Mouse.

'Fine thanks, Sergeant Halfpenny. But no time for idle chit chat with you.'

'I know, you're very busy, Q, so I'll make it quick.'

Cow Bag raised her eyebrows, still managing to look irritated.

'You'll keep what quick?'

'Look, Gayle,'

'Don't push it, Sergeant Halfpenny. It's Q to you.'

'All right, Q. We're all on the same side you know.'

'We...'

'Look,' Mouse continued quickly. 'I think we started off on the wrong foot and I want to remedy that. How do you fancy going for a drink after work tomorrow? I know you work long hours, but I can wait until you've finished.'

'I'm off tomorrow afternoon. That's such a shame, eh?'

Mouse ignored the sarcasm.

'Okay then, how about Saturday or Sunday?'

'Nope. That doesn't work either. I'm going away tomorrow night and won't be back until Sunday morning. I'll have far too much to do to meet up with you.'

This was getting interesting, thought Mouse. 'That sounds exciting. You off anywhere nice then, Q. Got some sort of secret assignation that you don't want us oiks to know about?'

Cow Bag's face turned to thunder and she didn't attempt to hide her feelings this time.

'How dare you. How very dare you! For someone as common as muck, you will never understand what it's like to be held in such high esteem and to...'

'Go on, Q, and to what?'

'I'm going where the likes of you will never see.'

'Oh, really?' Mouse added, revelling in the fact that she'd wound her up.

'Yes really. It's a very exclusive spa hotel and they're extremely fussy about their clientele. Get your own life Sergeant Halfpenny and stop poking your nose in matters that don't concern you.'

'Well I hope you and your date have a wonderful time, Q. Make sure you don't do anything I wouldn't do.'

'I'm not going on a date! I'm going for a well-earned break!'

'Whatever you say, Q. Cheerio.'

Cow Bag ignored her, but Mouse could see she was struggling to keep her temper, so job done. Now all she had to do was discover which spa hotel they were going to. As it turned out, it wasn't that difficult.

*****

The trip to the jewellers didn't go as planned. 'Thank you,' the man behind the counter said politely when Mouse gave him the paperwork and sixty pounds. 'But the outstanding amount is eighty pounds, not sixty.'

Knowing what the boss was like with money, Mouse didn't need to see proof, but she asked to anyway. Sure enough, the sales receipt said eighty and not sixty. 'Can you do him a deal and do it for sixty, please?'

He looked at her as if she'd just farted in his shop.

'Madam, the outstanding balance is eighty pounds please. How would you like to proceed?'

She knew exactly how she'd like to proceed but didn't express her thoughts. 'Give me ten minutes to go to the bank and I'll get the rest of the money.'

Bloody typical. That's another twenty quid he would owe her, on top of the fiver for two months' coffee money, and she bought most of his chocolate. This had to stop.

Back at the jewellers fifteen minutes later, Mouse paid the remaining twenty pounds and the man behind the counter put the necklace in a beautiful, black velvet presentation box and gift wrapped it in gold coloured shiny paper with a gold bow.

'Thank you, Madam. Would you like me to add thirty, instead of twenty pounds to the receipt for your inconvenience?'

'Err, that's most kind of you,' Mouse replied. 'But just put the twenty on it, please.'

'Certainly, Madam. But nobody would know.'

'Except me,' she said, and swanned out of the shop doing her superior moral high ground walk. Then she remembered that she planned on blackmailing a senior officer and the stuck-up cow who just happened to be a warrant officer. Either of them could do irreparable damage to her career if they so wished. Mouse remembered Earl's words from Saturday afternoon when he told her that the worst had already happened to her. He was right, too. She'd lost the love of her life and didn't give a shit. And she kept on trying to convince herself of that until the brigadier returned to the office for his lunch.

He came in whistling so all must have gone well.

'Good meeting, Sir?' she asked as she put a plate containing his sandwich and the Kit Kat on his desk with one hand, and his coffee with another.

'Oh, yes, Mouse. Did you get the present?'

'Yes, Sir and the card.'

He rubbed his hands together as he thanked her, then took a bite out of his sandwich.

'It was eighty quid, Sir, not sixty like you said. The card was three pound fifty and with your sandwich, the chocolate and the unpaid money for the coffee fund. I doubt I'll be able to eat for the rest of this month, Sir.'

The boss spluttered tuna, cucumber and bread out of his mouth back onto his plate and let out a roar of laughter.

'Okay, okay. Point taken, Mouse.' He stood up and did what they called in the Sergeants' Mess, the Sandhurst Shuffle. Patting down all his pockets, he must have realised he didn't have any cash on him. 'I'll go to the bank and settle up with you as soon as I've finished my lunch. And thank you. You go above and beyond and I appreciate it.'

He was a decent bloke and she couldn't be mad at him for long and there was the fact that he was a brigadier and Mouse a sergeant, money or no money.

'Then how about I give you some money and you keep a record of what you buy and let me know when you need a top up?'

'Sounds like a great idea, Sir. Thanks,' said Mouse, and the boss beamed at her. He was a bloke after all and needed training, whatever his rank.

'So now I have to think of what to do with Mrs Riley this weekend to make her birthday special.'

'How about taking her on a nice break to a spa hotel, Sir? I heard Q Johnson talking about that and she said there's a lovely one that's quite exclusive, but I can't remember the name of it. I'll ask her if you like?'

'Ah, no need for that, Mouse. It's the Hambleton Oasis outside Haselmere. Very popular place and Mrs Riley talked me into taking her last Easter and she hated it!' He laughed. 'Full of yuppies and people who are no better than they should be, according to Mrs Riley.' He stopped to chew some of the sandwich before adding. 'She wouldn't be seen dead in there again.'

'Perhaps the Ivy then, Sir. Nice pre-theatre dinner then a show and maybe overnight at the Savoy?'

'Hmm, not sure about the Savoy but dinner and a show will go down very well. Good thinking.'

She could see he was itching to read the new reports on his desk and wanted him to go to the bank. 'Will there be anything else, Sir?'

'No thanks. Let me go through this lot, then the bank before it closes.'

He was as good as his word, and less than an hour later, Mouse had received what he owed her, plus twenty-five quid petty cash money. 'And remember to tell me when you need a top up.'

'Don't you worry about that, Sir.'

She was glad she hadn't succumbed to temptation and hadn't colluded with the man in the jewellery shop.

*****

After a busy four days in work, Mouse was in her room in the mess on Thursday evening, wondering what to take for her overnight stay in the Hambleton Oasis the following night. If her luck was in, she'd see Cow Bag and the cheating brigadier and would be able to start planning her future. Mouse knew what she was doing wasn't right, but neither were they and although two wrongs didn't make a right, she remembered that she didn't give a shit so went ahead with her plan.

Despite what Cow Bag had said, it had been easy to book a room. She gave her name and agreed to the supplement for the single room.

'We only have one deluxe single room left, madam.'

'Okay, I'll take it.'

There was silence for a few seconds before he responded. 'That'll be two hundred and thirty pounds, Madam, plus thirty-seven pounds for the single room supplement.'

'Like I said, I'll take it.' Mouse tried to hide her surprise at the price they quoted and had to resist making a sarcastic comment about buying shares in the place. Two hundred and thirty quid! She'd have to take money out of her savings for this one.

'But it does include breakfast, Madam,' he added, as if that justified the extortionate price.

These hoity toity people must be stark raving bonkers if that was the usual price they paid for a night away, four star or not. Knowing she could have had a weekend in Wales with her family, a few nights out, treated them to dinner and still have change, didn't help her mood. But this would hopefully be worth the price in exchange for a posting to Hong Kong.

If everything went well, she'd be able to dine out on this story with family and close friends in years to come.

*****

Mouse had a leisurely Friday morning then made her way to Waterloo Station in the afternoon, from where she got a train directly to Haslemere. It was mid-afternoon, so the trains were emptier than usual, and it was good to get a window seat so she could watch the world go by and daydream.

The booking agent had given her rough directions to the hotel and Mouse knew it was too far to walk so she got in one of the few taxis waiting outside the station.

'Hambleton Oasis, please.'

The driver just looked at her, no doubt wondering if she could afford it.

'How long will it take?'

'The Hambleton Oasis you say?'

'That's right, yeah.'

'Okey dokey. It's about ten minutes.'

She settled in and it wasn't long before they were in the countryside.

'The hotel's between two valleys,' he said, 'but it's outside one of the National Trust Walks so you might see the walkers in the distance, but not hear them. So I'm told anyway. Not that I could afford to stay there on my wages.'

'It sounds delightful,' Mouse responded. 'But you're right, it is expensive.'

'It used to belong to one of the gentry but their ancestors couldn't afford it so they sold it to the Oasis hotel group.' Like most taxi drivers, he chatted during the rest of the ride, about the local area, the state of the country and that favourite British topic, the weather.

Mouse got a look at the place as they came over a hill and, from a distance, it did look like an English gentry ancestral home.

'Here we are then,' he said, as he pulled up outside the hotel.

A man dressed in black trousers, a shirt and long black jacket with burgundy borders and cuffs opened the door.

'Madam,' he said swooping an arm dramatically to indicate she should leave the vehicle.

'Thank you,' Mouse replied, before turning to the driver to pay. When she looked around, the employee was already holding her bag and she followed him into the hotel.

The checking-in process was very efficient with the receptionist checking her Access card details were the same that she'd given over the phone.

'Dinner's from 6.30 to 9pm Ms Halfpenny. Shall I book you a table?'

'It's Mrs Halfpenny actually'.

He nodded his head in acknowledgement.

'And yes please. Could you book me a table for 8pm, just for one and do you have a quiet table, say in a corner?'

'Of course, Mrs Halfpenny. Consider it done. Daniel will show you to your room.'

'Thank you,' she replied with a smile. 8pm was a bit late for dinner for Mouse but she knew that dinner times were later in the Officers Messes and some of them preferred to eat late so she hoped this would be the case with Brigadier

Harding-Brown and Cow Bag and that she would surprise them. Others might have doubts about whether they had chosen the right hotel or whether the people she wanted to spy on would actually turn up, but not Mouse. She had a gut instinct and was absolutely one hundred percent certain that Cow Bag and the brigadier would check into this hotel. In the time between now and dinner, Mouse intended to quickly settle into her room and make the most of the facilities the hotel had to offer.

She was determined to get her money's worth, and she did so, in more ways than one.

She followed Daniel as instructed and they got a lift to the top floor. They walked to the end of the corridor and he unlocked the door to the last room.

'The lights, Madam,' he flicked the switches, showing her which one was for the bathroom and those for the bedroom. Then he walked to the window and opened the curtains. 'I'm sure you'll agree it's beautiful and most relaxing?'

'It is beautiful, yes,' she said, as she looked out of the window at the rolling countryside.'

'Complimentary slippers are in the wardrobe, Madam, and there is also a dressing gown for your use. Enjoy your stay and press number one to call Reception,' he nodded to the phone, 'if you need anything.'

'Thank you, Daniel,' said Mouse, getting into the swing of things. He seemed to be waiting for something.

'Oh yes,' she muttered, almost forgetting the protocol. She fished two fifty pence pieces out of her pocket and gave them to him.

'Thank you, Madam,' Daniel said as he left the room.

Mouse unpacked her overnight kit and looked in the mini fridge. The prices were extortionate and, yet again, she wondered at the sort of people who were willing to pay ridiculous prices for crisps, nuts and tiny bottles of wine and spirits. She took some of the provisions out of the fridge and put in the sandwich, can of coke and Twix that she'd picked up from the station at Waterloo. She read the hotel guide.

She could use the indoor pool without further charge, and also the sauna, steam room and Jacuzzi. She would obviously have to pay if she wanted a massage, facial, or any other treatment from the *world class* beauty therapist.

Mouse decided she'd go for a long walk the following morning, but for now would check out the swimming pool and sauna, then perhaps shower before a session in the Jacuzzi. She changed into her swimming costume and put on the soft white dressing gown that was emblazoned with the *Oasis* logo, grabbed the towel, and wash bag. About to leave the room she changed her mind and picked up her small camera from the chair. It was rare for her to stay in such a luxurious place, so she wanted to take some photographs to show her family next time she saw them

It was lovely and warm in the pool area and as she entered, a man got out of the pool, put on one of the hotel dressing gowns, and left. Mouse was the only one there and she intended to make the most of it. She took a few photos and now being a competent swimmer, dived in. Swimming breaststroke, she kept her head under water for as long as she could. She continued swimming as she broke the surface and, not the fastest of swimmers, did a slow twenty lengths of the twenty-five-metre pool before stopping for a rest. She pushed off the side with her feet and floated around on her back for a few minutes, before deciding to do some more lengths. Thirty minutes later she was pleasantly tired and played around in the pool until she caught her breath. She tried a few handstands and forward and backward rolls and wondered how on earth synchronized swimming teams could look so graceful and elegant, when she looked like a baby elephant or a distressed spider.

Mouse dried off, put the comfy dressing gown on over her costume, and made her way to the sauna area where she took a few more photographs. There appeared to be a reception, but it wasn't manned by anyone and a sign read *Back in ten minutes.* Unfortunately, it didn't have a time on it, so Mouse had no idea whether that had been placed one minute or nine minutes ago. Never having been in this hotel or a sauna before she didn't know the protocol, but assumed it was just like the pool and you went in when you wanted. Had she seen the bookings folder on the chair she would have known different, but a hotel towel had been tossed on the chair and it covered it. It was all very quiet, and Mouse felt the need to tiptoe to the sauna area. It looked like a large wooden hut, but she could see there were windows on each side. She peeked through one and did a double take. Mouse ducked down, to give her brain time to process what she'd just seen. There was now absolutely no doubt in her mind that Brigadier Harding-Brown and Cow Bag were having an illicit affair. She smiled to herself. Did she have the guts to go through with it? Hell yes! Putting on what she thought was a neutral expression, Mouse pushed open the door.

'What the hell!' she said before quickly aiming her camera and catching them both in an uncompromising position.

She thought she gave a good impression of being suitably surprised and their reaction was priceless. Their lips were still locked together. Both sets of eyes opened at the same time and their mouths hurriedly separated. The brigadier dropped his hand from Cow Bag's breast, and she pulled her towel up hastily.

'Afternoon, Sir, Ma'am. Fancy seeing you here.'

'Of all the...' Q Johnson started, and Mouse knew she was in for a proper bollocking, although Q wasn't in any position to tell her off and no way was she going to take it.

'Of all the what? Tell me you weren't going to have a go at me when I've caught you with a senior officer, and a married one at that. And you act like you're better than the rest of us...'

'Sergeant Halfpenny,' said the brigadier. 'It's not how it looks. Give me that camera.'

She could tell from the look on his face and his response that he was most definitely married. 'Don't insult my intelligence, Sir. Does your wife know you're here? And no, I won't give you my camera.'

He didn't respond. 'No, of course she doesn't, poor woman.'

'How can a sergeant afford...'

Mouse interrupted before she could finish the sentence. 'I don't believe you at times. I've caught you in a compromising position and all you're concerned about is how I can afford to stay in a place like this? Incredible.'

'Sergeant Halfpenny, this is to go no further,' said the brigadier.

'Does it really matter, Giles?' asked his lover putting a hand on his thigh. 'If we're going to be together you have to tell her sometime. Maybe it's time?'

'You know she's ill, darling, and this will make it worse. I told you, as soon as Henrietta goes off to uni I'll tell her, and we can be together forever.'

'Oh yeah,' Mouse interrupted. 'Do you think he's really going to leave his wife for you? Honestly? If so, you're more naive than I realised. You're his bit on the side, Gayle. He's probably got one in every port, city or whatever.'

There was a tiny flicker in the brigadier's eyes that made Mouse think she was spot on. But no matter. She needed to cut to the chase and get on with business.

'I think we ought to leave,' Cow Bag said to her lover. 'I can't stand being in the same place as her for any longer.'

'I think you ought to leave, *Gayle*,' Mouse emphasised the name to annoy the warrant officer, but the woman hardly appeared to notice. 'I want a private chat with the brigadier.'

'Well that's not happening. Who do you think you are?'

'Actually, it is happening, Gayle. You know as a senior NCO, I feel duty bound to report this to my senior officers. After all, isn't it our duty to maintain high moral standards in the British Army and to lead by example? And if you deny it...' She gave her camera a little shake.

'Oh God.' The brigadier put his head in his hands and Mouse realised what a spineless git he was.

'But like I said, I want to have a private chat with the brigadier to see if we can avoid any disciplinary action in this case.'

'Disciplinary action?' Cow Bag asked.

'Yes indeed, Gayle. So can you leave us in peace, please?' Mouse saw no need to forget her own manners. Either that, or something inside her wanted to wind her up even more. 'Tell the receptionist not to let anyone in for fifteen minutes and go back to your room. If I suspect you of listening outside, I'll return to the MOD and make sure the press get hold of this story straight away.'

She could see by their faces that they knew she was serious, so Q gave the brigadier a final look and left. Mouse waited for a minute then opened the door. There was nobody about except the beautician, now returned to the reception area, and she gave Mouse a questioning look. Mouse ignored it, went back into the sauna and sat on the bench opposite the brigadier.

'What do you want?' he asked.

'A posting to Hong Kong, Sir,' she said with a sweet smile. 'Can you fix that for me?'

'You already know there aren't any vacancies.'

'Well that's such a shame, Sir. But I daresay they'll be looking for a new deputy commander soon, when the Army Board decides to remove you from post. And a new PA to CGS. What a palaver. I don't suppose my boss will be too impressed either, having to answer all those questions from the press, especially as you two are such good friends. Well never mind. At least I tried.' She got up to leave, knowing he would do anything to save his reputation and career but Mouse was unsure which was the most important to him. Probably the career due to the hefty pension on completion.

'All right, all right. But I'm not sure I'll be able to move my own PA. That might be a little difficult.'

A sixth sense kicked in. 'So she's another bit on the side is she, that you can't afford to upset? I don't suppose Mrs Harding-Brown or Q Johnson knows about her, either?'

'Sergeant Halfpenny…' He reached over to touch her, and Mouse recoiled.

'Never mind Sergeant Halfpenny, Sir. You're a brigadier and I know you have some influence. You have one week and if you haven't sorted out my Hong Kong posting by then, I won't keep my mouth shut. And also, if you try anything funny to blacken my name, remember I have proof that I can use.' She shook the camera.

'Okay,' he said with a defeated look. 'I'll be in touch.' And with that he got up off the bench and left.

That was the last time Mouse saw them both at the hotel. She had a pleasant dinner that evening and a long walk the following morning before checking out, but instead of feeling ecstatic knowing her plan had come to fruition, she felt soiled and disappointed with herself knowing that she'd decided to lower her own standards by blackmailing others to get her own way. *It's done now girl,* she thought to herself, *so you just need to get on with it.*

It was a bittersweet moment when the posting came through the following week. Hong Kong in two months' time as the PA to the Deputy Commander. So she'd have to work for the randy brigadier for a year when his posting would be up, but she could handle that. She was going to be near Graham and Grace and get to live in one of the most exciting and vibrant cities in the world (so she'd heard). Mouse put all thoughts of her deviousness out of her head and dared to look forward to her future.

Chapter 4 – Hong Kong

Mouse felt ready for the next phase of her life as she boarded the British Caledonian flight at Heathrow airport. She'd heard somewhere that up to one hundred seats were allocated weekly for troops flying to the Far East. She noticed the stairs on the other side of the massive 747 then her eyes wandered towards the seats on the left which looked far more luxurious than she'd seen in any plane she'd flown on before. A pretty stewardess pulled the curtain across.

'Turn right,' she said looking down her nose at her. *Stuck up cow, thought Mouse* as she showed her boarding pass to another stewardess.

'58C,' this woman said with a smile. 'You're right down the back.'

'Thank you,' Mouse said with a smile as she headed to her seat. As she sat and waited for the aircraft to fill she looked around and played 'spot the squaddie' as she did so. A family with a baby and a young, stroppy toddler sat two rows in front of her. The young mother already looked harassed as the baby cried loudly and the toddler kept asking for something to eat and drink. As the husband put their bags in the overhead locker, he looked directly at Mouse and winked. *Cheeky beggar,* she thought, but it made her laugh and she couldn't hide her smile. There were a few other families who looked like the husband was military, but other than that, there didn't appear to be many soldiers on this flight.

The pilot welcomed the passengers on board and introduced the cabin crew, then they were good to go. As the plane took off and the land below started to disappear, the baby two rows in front howled loudly and a smell hit Mouse's nostrils. It was that bad she grabbed the sick bag from the back of the seat in front and heaved into it. As soon as the fasten seatbelt sign went off, the young mother, carrying the screaming baby and nappy changing kit, made her way past Mouse to the nearest toilet. She had a fresh whiff of the baby's soiled nappy, which made her heave for the second time. The man in the window seat gave Mouse a dirty look and harrumphed before rustling his newspaper. She gave him an apologetic look, which he chose to ignore. *This is going to be a long flight*, she thought, as she watched the friendly stewardess approach. She stopped and bent towards Mouse.

'Would you like to get your bag and follow me please, Mrs Halfpenny, I have a new seat for you.'

Mouse didn't hesitate and was doing internal cartwheels as she followed the woman into the business-class section of the aircraft.

'It's your lucky day,' said the stewardess. 'I'm sure you'll be very comfortable in this seat.'

The seats were wider and were in rows of two-three-two instead of three-four-three where she'd been sitting. There was a bigger TV screen on the back of the seat in front of her, and the chairs reclined without spoiling the viewing. On her right was a large armrest and a drinks holder. The older woman in the window seat next to Mouse had a black eye mask on and was breathing heavily. Mouse smiled to herself as she took her book out of her bag – she could get used to this lifestyle.

'Wine, Madam?' asked a stewardess who Mouse hadn't seen earlier. Before she could respond, the stewardess added, 'or would you prefer champagne?'

Is the Pope a Catholic? 'Champagne would be lovely, thanks,' she replied in a voice she hoped conveyed that she was used to sitting up front and drinking champagne. The woman poured the drink and handed it to Mouse, then gave her a small bag of nuts and a cloth napkin.

'I'll be back to refill your glass before we serve dinner. Enjoy the flight.'

'Oh I will, thank you,' she replied, still hardly believing her luck.

She wasn't so lucky on the second flight from Dubai to Hong Kong, so she plugged in her Walkman to listen to George Michael and Kylie. As the plane landed at Kai Tak Airport, Mouse was shattered. From the bleary-eyed looks on all of their faces, so were the other passengers who had been on board. She was still very excited that the Army had sent her somewhere so exotic, and as she stepped out of the door, was hit by a heat that resembled that of a fan oven, and a smell that hit her nostrils and made her heave once again. The last time she'd smelled anything as bad was when the freezer had broken while she was away with Guy and everything had turned putrid by the time they returned.

'It does get better,' a Chinese passenger said to her, 'honestly.'

She certainly hoped so. Mouse and the other military personnel and their dependants were chivvied through the customs channel and out onto the street. The others were told to get on a bus but Mouse was asked to wait. Graham was coming to meet her, so she was surprised a few minutes later when a car pulled up and out got a Chinese man wearing British Army uniform bearing corporal stripes.

'Hi, I'm Soo Key,' he said. 'One of CBF's drivers. You must be Sergeant Halfpenny?'

'Hello. Yes, that's right, I'm Mouse Halfpenny. Pleased to meet you?'

'Mouse, like the rodent?'

'Yup. It's just a nickname. Where's Graham?'

'He's, aah, been caught up and asked me to come and get you?'

'What do you mean caught up? What's happened? Is he...?'

Soo Key laughed. 'He said you'd ask lots of questions and to tell you there's nothing to worry about, he'll explain later.'

Although tired after a day spent travelling and her body clock being all over the place, her fuddled brain still told her something wasn't right. If nothing was wrong, why didn't Soo Key simply say that Graham had to work, instead of telling her not to worry?

'Seriously, he's okay.'

CBF's driver must have seen the concern on her face and was trying to placate her. Although heavily accented, his English was perfect and Mouse was grateful he was trying to make her feel better. And he'd given up his spare time to do a favour for a friend. She liked the man already and decided to let it go. As Mouse went to pick up her heavy cases off the trolley, Soo Key took over.

'You get in the car, Sarge, I'll get these.'

'Oh, thanks, and call me Mouse, please.'

He nodded and a few minutes later they were on their way.

Neon lights lit up the buildings like gigantic Christmas decorations, only it wasn't Christmas and many of the lights were advertising brands, mostly for the latest electronic gadgets. It was like a bright, tall, brick jungle, and although she was tired, the excitement of being in a city that felt totally alien and exotic kept her awake. As they approached the cross-harbour tunnel, some of the lights dimmed and the tall, bright buildings became less and less. Even though they were in an air-conditioned car, there was still a faint smell of fumes in the tunnel. Hidden now from the outside world, the only lights were those of other vehicles. The low buzz of the air conditioning and the hum of the car engine were the only sounds and Mouse suddenly felt overwhelmingly tired. She eventually lost the fight to keep her eyes open.

She didn't even know she'd fallen into a deep sleep until she felt someone shaking her arm. Totally disorientated, she looked at the man sitting next to her, taking a few seconds to remember she was now in Hong Kong.

'We're here.'

As she opened the door and stepped outside the car she looked at the building lit up in front of her. It looked like a gin bottle turned upside down.

'Welcome to HMS Tamar, your home for the next three years. I'll get your bags.'

'Thanks, Soo Key, that's really....' Mouse was cut off mid-sentence.

'It's all right, mate. I'm on it.'

She turned at the voice, knowing she'd recognise it anywhere. 'Graham!' Mouse flung herself at her brother and hugged him fiercely.

'I can't breathe,' he laughed, but he took her embrace in his stride until she eventually let him go. Now fully awake, Mouse started babbling. 'How's Grace and my gorgeous niece? When will I see them? Do you live far from here? What's the...'

'Okay, okay. All in good time.'

His frown gave it away and Mouse waited to hear whatever was bothering him.

'What is it, Gray? They are both okay aren't they?'

'Elfie's fine, Michelle. You won't recognise...'

'And Grace?' Mouse interrupted, watching as her brother's head drooped and a frown crossed his brow. 'Graham, please! You're worrying me now.'

Soo Key coughed. They'd both forgotten he was there. 'Do you need any help with those bags?'

'Sorry, mate.' Graham replied. 'I'm really grateful to you for collecting my sister.'

'Yeah, I am too, Soo Key. Thanks and we'll see you again.'

'No problem. I hope you enjoy it here.'

'I'm sure I will,' Mouse replied, trying her best to be polite but wanting him to leave so her brother could tell her what the hell was going on.

'Graham?' she said as the car door closed, and Soo Key drove away.

'Don't panic but Grace is in hospital.'

'Oh no! What's happened? Has she had a relapse? Is she going to be...'

'Okay, calm down. She's not well and they're running some tests to determine what's wrong.'

'Is it anything to do with the accident? Has something happened?' Mouse stopped talking and put a hand to her mouth, trying her best not to chew her fingers. This was the only way she could stop herself from asking incessant questions and let her brother finish explaining.

'They're doing some tests and say we should get the results by the end of this week.' His head was still down, and he looked defeated. Mouse put her arms around her brother for a second time and held him tight. They stayed like that for a long time, standing outside the building that housed the British Forces Headquarters, and accommodation for many of its employees.

Eventually Graham pulled away and said, 'Shall we get you up to your room, Mouse, then I'll explain further.'

She agreed, hardly noticing her surroundings as she worried about her brother, one of her best friends, and her lovely little niece as she wondered what the future held for their family. Every time life threw them a safety net, it seemed like some quirk of fate was determined to take it back off them. Life could be so unfair at times.

The Warrant Officer and Sergeants Mess was on the 22nd floor of the building. Graham briefly explained that the headquarters covered floors ten to fourteen and the floors up to number twenty-two housed the junior ranks, senior NCOs and Officers Messes. She wasn't taking in any of the details Graham gave to her; partly because she was more tired than she'd ever been in her whole life, but mainly because of worry about Grace. Mouse could have been anywhere in the world, but all she wanted at that moment was to see her sister-in-law.

'When can I see her?'

'Tomorrow. You need to get a good night's sleep.'

Mouse grunted an acknowledgement, knowing he was right. 'Okay,' she said, 'I'll see you tomorrow. Night, night.' Now in her room, Mouse unpacked her overnight bag and used the toilet in the small bathroom that was attached to it. *The Army are certainly coming into the 20th Century here,* she thought, pleased that she wouldn't have to traipse all the way along a corridor to use a bathroom, as she had in previous messes. She put on a nightshirt and crawled into her already made up bed, resigned to the fact that worrying about Grace, her brother, and Elfie would keep her awake for most of the night. However, as her body clock was all over the place, even if she'd wanted to stay awake, Mouse would have been unable to. Seconds after her head hit the pillow, she was totally out of it.

Ringing woke Mouse and she sat up and looked around, totally disorientated. When she remembered where she was, she quickly found the phone on the bedside locker to the left of her bed. Unsure of the protocol, her military training kicked in as she picked up the receiver.

'Good morning, Sergeant Halfpenny speaking.'

There was a chuckle on the other end of the line. 'It's afternoon actually and I'll be there to get you in twenty minutes. Give you time to have a shower and find some kit to wear.'

'Afternoon? Graham? How's Grace?'

'She's home, Mouse. They discharged her from DKMH.'

'DKMH?'

'You know, the Duchess of Kent Military Hospital, come on, Mouse, you should know that!'

She did know about the hospitals that were exclusive for military personal and their dependants, but in her defence, she had just woken up, felt like shit, and didn't know if she was on this earth or Fuller's earth!

'Give me a break, Graham. My brain isn't functioning yet, and I need a coffee. I'll have to go into the mess dining hall…'

'Have a look around your rooms, Mouse. I think you'll be pleasantly surprised. Now go and get ready. We'll meet you downstairs in twenty?'

'We? I thought you said Grace was sleeping?'

'Me and Elfie. She can't wait to see her auntie.'

'Yay!' Mouse replied before hanging up. The desire to see her niece, and eventually Grace, as well as Graham, gave her all the incentive she needed to get a move on.

She was impressed that there was a fridge in her room, and tea and coffee making facilities. There was also a small room off the bedroom area with a settee and desk. A few booklets and some pieces of laminated paper were on the desk. One of the booklets was the Sergeants Mess rules. There was also a room inventory and a note in large print explaining that the bathroom was shared with her neighbour (on the other side of the bathroom) and when using it, each occupant was to lock the other door from inside, thereby preventing the person in the room opposite from entering. *Fair enough,* thought Mouse. This was the nearest she had had to her own bathroom, so she was very happy with the facilities so far.

She made herself a coffee and spent as much time in the shower as would allow her to be ready on time to see her brother and little Elfie.

New posting, new country, new life. Mouse had been excited during the last few days but knowing Grace was ill had now put a dampener on it. She had a few days before having to start the induction process and take over her new job, so she intended to spend as much time as possible with her family. But the fact that Grace had now been discharged from hospital surely meant that there was nothing seriously wrong with her and she was on the mend? Mouse tried not to let her optimism get the better of her, just in case.

She opened the door to her room and stepped outside into the corridor. Even with her miserable sense of direction, she was able to find the lift lobby. It was signposted – in case of fire, Mouse presumed – and she only had to walk along one corridor, around a corner, then down another. She pressed the button and waited.

The doors opened and a man walked out, totally ignoring Mouse.

'Good afternoon,' she said, cheerily. The old Chinese man looked at her, nodded, then grudgingly said, 'Good afternoon,' in heavily accented English. He was dressed in black trousers and a white shirt, so Mouse rightly assumed he was likely to be one of the mess staff.

The two men in the lift smirked as she entered. One was a warrant officer, and the other, dressed in a smart civvy suit, looked to Mouse like one of the higher up civil servants she'd seen walking around the MOD in London.

'Hi, I'm Neil Mitchum, Chief Clerk J1 and I look after you girls in the Command Group, too. This is Civ Sec. You must be Sergeant Michelle Halfpenny?'

'That's right, Sir, Mouse Halfpenny. Nice to meet you,' she replied shaking hands with them both. Mouse had a fleeting thought that being referred to as a *girl* in this day and age was more than a little patronising.

'Well, Mouse, you'll find a lot of people here in Hong Kong are vertical commuters and, like most commuters, don't bother with conversation when they're travelling.'

'Even common courtesies?'

'Even the basics. You'll soon get used to it. You've got a few days to look around before starting work I'm told, and I know your brother is helping. Beth, CBF's PA, will help you with the orientation when you start work because the general's on leave at the mo.'

The lift stopped and Civ Sec nodded to Mouse before exiting. Warrant Officer 2 Mitchum held the door as he continued chatting.

'If you make the most of Hong Kong you'll love it. Don't make the mistake of keeping yourself to yourself. Get out there and enjoy everything it has to offer. I would offer to show you around but I'm getting married next week and moving out of the mess.'

'Congratulations,' she replied, as a cleaning lady with a trolley approached the lift and Q Mitchum had to make the decision to get out or to stay. He hadn't stopped talking and as friendly as he seemed, Mouse was desperate to see Graham and Elfie and to hear what was going on with Grace.

'Right, this is my stop,' he said, stating the obvious. 'See you on Monday. Beth will come to your room at zero seven thirty hours. If you have any issues in the meantime that Graham can't handle, I'm in room 143.'

'Thanks, Q,' she replied, having no intention of bothering him before she started work the following week.

He put his hand up in a wave and disappeared. Mouse smiled at the cleaning lady as she entered the lift and the woman smiled back, nodding as she did so.

Without any further interruptions or stops, she got to the ground floor and the lift doors opened. Graham and Elfie were there to greet her.

Mouse hardly recognised the little girl standing in front of her. Last seen as a toddler, Elfie was now almost four years old. She wore a cute little dress, patterned with red flowers which matched her red sandals and the bow holding together the mass of blonde curls.

'Hello, Elfie,' Mouse said, wondering if the child would be shy around her. She needn't have concerned herself.

'Ley ho ma, Auntie Mouse,' said Elfie, before flinging her arms around Mouse's legs.

Mouse picked up her niece and hugged her, revelling in the clean and sweet smell of the innocent child.

'*Lay home a?*' she asked.

'It's Chinese,' said Elfie before Graham had a chance to respond. 'Mummy and Daddy said I'm going to be binwal. That means I know some Chinese words, Auntie Mouse. Why are you called Mouse? Don't you have a proper name? I like mice…' She continued rabbiting on for a while then asked to be put down.

'Squeak, squeak,' she said, screwing up her face as she imagined a mouse might. 'Can you make a sound like a mouse, Auntie Mouse?'

'Squeak, squeak,' Mouse responded, and Elfie laughed.

'I like you, Auntie Mouse, you're funny. All of my friend's aunties are people. I'm the only one with an auntie who's a mouse.'

'I'm not actually a real mouse.'

'Oh,' said Elfie, disappointed. 'I still like you though. We have to go home 'cause Mummy's not well. I'm still going to be binwal though.'

'Elfie,' said Graham as Mouse gave him a questioning look. 'Let's get you to kindergarten.'

'But I want to stay with Auntie Mouse.'

'You'll see Auntie Mouse later, Elfie, before you go to bed.'

'But you'll all go out and leave me with Ack-O,' said Elfie, her lip starting to quiver.

'We'll get Ack-O to make us dinner and we'll eat at home. Then Auntie Mouse can play with you before you go to bed.'

'Hooray! I'm going to tell all of my friends about my Auntie Mouse. Can you come and play with us now?'

'No she can't,' said Graham. 'Now let's get you off to kindergarten before we're in trouble for being late.'

Elfie put herself in between Graham and Mouse, holding hands with them both. They walked the short distance to the kindergarten like this, Mouse not yet realising that this would be impossible to do in lots of Hong Kong places due to five million people occupying a city that was originally intended for a lot less.

After dropping Elfie off, they made their way towards the bridge walkway en route to Graham and Grace's married quarters in the old Victoria Barracks area, known locally as Victoria Bing Fong, Wanchai. It didn't take Mouse long to become irritated by the masses of people they had to dodge on the bridge walkway.

'Is it a bank holiday or something?'

'Eh?'

'Why are there so many people about? Are they all off work or something?'

'It's always busy here, Mouse, and in Kowloon. There are over five million in Hong Kong, and it's one of the most densely populated places on earth. But I daresay you'll discover all of this on your newbies' brief. That's if you have one. I didn't but Soo Key told me everything I need to know.'

She tried to keep up with Graham, doing her best to dodge some of the local populace as she did so. She should have tried to keep tabs on the route they were taking but trying to listen, dodge and take in the newness of everything was too much for her.

'Oi, steady!' As they entered the Hutchison House building, two women would have walked into her had Mouse not dodged them at the last moment. 'Are you blind or something?' she muttered under her breath.

They ignored her and carried on walking.

'Well that was a bit rude.'

'Get used to it, Mouse. Some of the locals call us gweilo or gweipos which roughly translates as white ghost. That means they can't see us so will walk into us if we don't move.'

'Well of all the…'

'You'll get used to it. Come on, this way.'

They walked through Hutchison House and entered the quieter Pacific Place, an upmarket mall. Mouse didn't have to slow down to notice the shops, the majority of which were expensive designer outlets such as Gucci, Prada, and Louis Vitton. The vibe was entirely different to what it had been as a variety of people dressed in designer gear ambled around.

'This way. We're nearly there.'

She followed her brother up an escalator, keeping to the right as she would have in London. At the top and to the right there were large glass doors indicating the entrance to a Marriott Hotel. At a glance, the lobby looked large and expensive.

'Wow!'

'I know. Sorry we haven't got time to do the tourist thing today. I'll show you around more tomorrow if you like?'

'Let's see what Grace wants to do.'

Graham knew his wife wasn't up to sightseeing, so said nothing.

The humidity hit her as soon as they left the air-conditioned building and Mouse felt her top instantly clinging to her body.

'Yuck,' she said, pulling at her t-shirt and wiping her brow. 'How long before you get used to this?'

'Never.' Graham laughed. 'You just learn to live with it.'

They waited for the traffic lights to change then crossed the road.

'That's it,' said Graham, pointing to a building a few minutes' walk away. 'Dragon House.'

'Wow,' she replied. Although the building wasn't that tall compared to others she'd seen so far, it was the tallest married quarters she had ever seen. 'So you live on the eighteenth floor?'

'Yup.'

As they approached the building, three stray dogs ran up steps that Mouse hadn't noticed, on her left.

'Aargh, Graham.'

'It's okay, they're more frightened of you. Honestly,' he added when he saw the look on his sister's face.

The first two dogs approached warily, and Mouse recoiled in horror when she saw the third. 'Look at that, the poor thing.' It was limping because its hind right leg was broken and appeared to be hanging off.

'I've been trying to catch it to take it to a vet, but it doesn't trust people. I've fed them a few times, but they're still scared. I guess someone's been really cruel to them in the past.'

The dogs turned and Mouse saw an old man walking up the steps. The pack ran in the opposite direction.

'See what I mean? Come on.'

Mouse was amazed her brother was so blasé about the animals who were obviously suffering. He seemed to sense her disquiet.

'You'll see a lot worse than that here, trust me. You need to grow a thick skin, pretty quickly.'

Coming out of the lift at the 18th floor, Graham had his keys ready, but the door opened.

'Haro Mister and Missy.' The old-looking Chinese woman smiled.

'Ack-O, this is my sister, Mouse.'

'Haro, Mouse,' the woman replied with a smile. 'Ack-O,' she said, then, 'Busy.'

She walked back into the flat and they followed.

Grace was lying on a large sofa in the living room, her eyes closed. She opened them as soon as she heard her husband and sister-in-law and sat up as quickly as she could.

'Mouse.'

Grace stood up slowly and Mouse tried to hide her shock at how pale and frail she looked. She enveloped her in a gentle hug and Grace started crying. Unable to control herself, Mouse joined in, though she didn't yet know why she was in tears.

'Let's sit down.'

Mouse did as she was told, worried that her beautiful sister-in-law who was also one of her best friends had cancer, and they were going to tell her that Grace didn't have long to live.

'I have MS, Mouse and we are moving back to the UK.'

'MS? But I thought...' She didn't finish that sentence. 'What's MS?'

'It's a progressive disease that attacks the immune system,' said Graham. 'You can have all sorts of problems and...'

'They can treat it though, yes? And you'll get better, Grace?' Seeing the looks on their faces, Mouse already knew the answer. She bit her bottom lip to stop herself from talking to allow Grace to get a word in.

'It can be slowed down, Mouse, but it's not curable, unfortunately.'

'Oh that's awful. After all you've been through and now this. Life's so unfair at times. And you look so tired.'

Grace gave a little laugh. 'You're such a bloody drama queen! Yes, today's a bad day and I'm absolutely exhausted, that's one of the symptoms. My muscles are aching too, and it hurts when I look up to the light.'

'What! That's awful.'

'It's not like I'm going to die soon, Mouse. They have drugs that can help me and, hopefully, I'll live a long and happy life. But if we want Graham to pursue his career and live as normal a life as possible, I'm going to need help. So...'

'I'll leave the Army, Grace. You know you and Elfie come first, it's not a problem...'

'We've already discussed this,' Grace interrupted. 'We still need money to live on, Graham, and it'll be better in the long-term if you stay in.' She turned to Mouse. 'We both know he loves the Army and he's already got a posting to 17 Sport and Pass time Squadron, which is only half an hour's commute from my parents.'

Mouse laughed at the description of the Port and Maritime Squadron and it lessened the tension in the room. 'So will you live with your parents? Is that the plan?'

'Only to start with. My mother's already looking for houses for sale in the local area. We're going to buy, Mouse and we'll deal with Graham's future postings when the problem arises.'

'They've said I can stay there for three years at the minimum, so we'll give it a try. But if it doesn't work, Grace, I'm out.'

'I know,' she replied. But Mouse knew that look and if Grace wanted Graham to stay in the Army long term, that's what would happen.

'So now you know. Can we talk about something else for a while? All I seem to do is talk about my illness and I don't want to be defined by it. Tell me all about your job in London and the people, and I'll tell you everything I've learnt about Hong Kong.'

'I'm going to clean the car,' Graham said, knowing he would most likely be ignored as the friends had a proper catch up.

*****

The next few days were a whirlwind of activity with Graham showing Mouse around, accompanied by Grace when she felt up to it. Mouse also spent as much time as she could with Elfie, knowing that by the end of the following month, the family would be on a plane returning to the UK. The days flew by and it seemed like no time at all when there was a knock at her door at seven thirty hours, on the Monday morning.

'Hello, I'm Beth.' The staff sergeant held out her hand and Mouse shook it, as she left her room.

'I'm Mouse Halfpenny.'

'Pleased to meet you, Mouse.' Beth raised an eyebrow.

70

'I know. It's been a nickname since I was a child. Do you like it here?'

'Love it, love it, love it! Hong Kong has sooooo much to offer. It's totally different to anywhere I've ever been before and I think you'll be the same. I know you'll want to spend as much time with Graham, Grace and of course, little Elfie, until they leave, but I'll show you around after that if you like? You can come to my aerobics class with me, too, if you're into that sort of thing? Need to exercise so we can eat all the scrummy food without putting on weight! I'm posted in a few months too so want to make the most of the rest of my time here.'

'That sounds great. But everyone I meet seems to be leaving!'

'Grace was right-you are a drama queen, Mouse.' Beth laughed and Mouse thought her sister-in-law had a flaming cheek saying that to people she didn't even know.

They entered the lift and Beth pressed the button for floor eleven. 'This is going to be your office for the next few years,' she said, as the lift door opened. 'And if you play your cards right, they might even promote you to take over my job.'

Mouse simply smiled and followed Beth.

She'd expected something like the MOD's Main Building that was badly in need of refurbishment. Mouse remembered going to a bank's headquarters once, on an errand for the brigadier, and this reminded her of that building. Large double doors led into a plush looking waiting area that housed a comfortable three-seater settee, with two matching chairs and a coffee table displaying a number of magazines. There was a buffet-type cabinet against the wall upon which was sitting a state of the art coffee machine and a water cooler was in an alcove in the corner. *I'll probably have to keep this area clean and do the washing up,* thought Mouse.

'Very nice,' she said to Beth.

'And there's a bonus. We have our own cleaning lady for this area and she keeps it tidy and does the washing up.'

It was as though Beth had read her mind, but Mouse wasn't entirely satisfied with the arrangement. 'What about security?'

'The locals aren't our enemy, Mouse.' Beth folded her arms. 'Anyone who works in this building has gone through strenuous security checks. So I'm told anyway. Come on, let me show you where we work and the other departments on this floor. The general is away until the end of the week so I'll spend most of today catching up and you can read about the job and Hong Kong in general. Then tomorrow to Thursday I'll show you the ropes. Your boss is out of office until Thursday. He can be a bit, erm…'

'If you mean a randy old goat, Beth, I already know. I met him in London when I worked for DPR.'

'Don't sit on the fence, Mouse! So, he didn't try…'

'Not with me, no. But I got the impression that if he thought there was the slightest chance…Well you know what I mean.'

'Very perceptive. But you were right, so go easy. You know it was a shock to us all when Claire Reynolds discovered she was posted back to the UK, even though it was meant to be on promotion. We were all convinced that something was going on there and she seemed more surprised to be leaving than any of us. She's crap at her job and I had to intervene with Major Jennings to try to make him see sense. Luckily enough, the major's reached his ceiling and he's got a set of balls. Can you imagine the reputation of our Corps if they promote someone as lazy as she is? I wouldn't be able to show my face in this office again.'

'Well you're brave, putting your head above the parapet and stopping her promotion,' said Mouse, knowing she wouldn't have been able to do that. 'What was her reaction.'

'I just said what others were already thinking. Major Jennings told me he'd heard a number of people were talking about it, so he phoned records. Knowing a brigadier was involved, they did a mini promotion board, even though she's not qualified and has failed her promotion course twice. She's left now, so it's not a problem but even if she hadn't, you have to have the courage of your convictions, Mouse, don't you think?'

'Oh yeah, I agree entirely,' Mouse replied, making a mental note not to get on the wrong side of Beth during the short time they would be working together.

'And anyway, she didn't know that I had anything to do with it.'

'I see.' Mouse intended to keep her thoughts to herself when around Beth; as much as it was possible for her to do so.

Wasting no further time, they entered the office. It was large, with four workspaces, and doors at each end of it- leading to the boss's, Mouse presumed.

'That's your desk.' Beth pointed to the desk at the far right of the office. 'The ADC is next to you, then the MA, and that's my desk, next to the door to the general's office. The door next to yours leads into the Deputy Commander's. Follow me,' she said, now all business.

It was plush and large as Mouse had expected, with a long table to the right then a big sumptuous desk at the far end. To the left, there were two comfy-looking chairs and a coffee table. Mouse took all this in at a glance but her eyes were being drawn to the large windows and stunning view.

'That's Central District and from there the Mid-Levels. You can see the Furama Hotel there,' she pointed. 'I think Grace and Graham are going to do the sightseeing stuff with you, so I won't waste time pointing out all the landmarks. It's a lot to take in.'

It certainly was. Hong Kong was a concrete jungle, but it was also stunning, and Mouse had lost count of how many times she'd said, *wow*, since arriving. She already loved it here but also knew it wouldn't take long before she'd feel claustrophobic and get fed up with trying to avoid the large number of people.

'It can get a bit manic out there at times, that's why we've been given money towards a leave scheme. You can get away from it all when it gets too much for you.'

Yet again Beth seemed to have read her mind.

Beth chuckled. 'Most of us feel a bit overwhelmed for our first couple of weeks, Mouse. But you'll soon get used to it. It's like London, only more condensed and a better standard of living – for us I mean, not the locals.' She went on to explain that many local families lived in tiny living areas where they paid a fortune for the privilege due to lack of space.

Mouse was keen to get stuck into the job and felt her mind wandering.

'…That's why many of them don't even have cooking facilities and eat out all the time. You can visit the luxurious hotels and restaurants and eat and drink like a queen for a reasonable price.'

Alert again, that information was stored away for future use.

'Enough of this chit chat. Let's get on.'

Mouse raised her eyebrows as she followed Beth out of the office.

The general's office was even more sumptuous than the brigadier's with an en suite bathroom attached to it.

'CBF is the third most important man in Hong Kong and is actually part of the government here,' Beth explained, and Mouse was suitably impressed. 'He's a member of the Legislative Council which is the Hong Kong Government.'

'I see,' Mouse replied. She had never been into UK politics and certainly wasn't interested in those of Hong Kong.

'He has to attend a number of meetings and if you ever stand in for me or my successor, you'll need to learn all about them. Even working for DCBF you'll need to know who's who in the local government, in order to avoid embarrassing yourself or our country's interests. He is also the Major General, Brigade of Gurkhas, MGBG as we call it, so you'll quite often see the Gurkha Major popping in and out of the office. He's the guy who has the general's ear about everything to do with Gurkhas and can…'

Mouse zoned out. She was getting bored now and felt Beth was bigging up the people and situation, just to make herself or others sound more important than they actually were. She had no intention of getting on the wrong side of the woman she needed help from so put on her best *you are so fascinating* face while letting her mind wander. She started thinking about Brigadier Harding-Brown and hoped she would be able to work for him considering the circumstances of her posting. Knowing what he was truly like, there was no way she could respect the man, but she did respect his rank. Once again she told herself that he must have once been decent in order to reach the rank of brigadier. He was a charmer, but his luck would have run out long before now had he relied purely on charm to get to one star.

'Your boss lives in a sumptuous quarter in Stanley Fort. Less than an hour's drive away from here. That's where the resident infantry battalion are based too. So that's about it for now.' Beth's mention of her own new boss returned her to the present. 'Grab a brew and start going through these.'

Looking at the pile of papers Beth had just handed her, Mouse knew she'd need more than one strong coffee to stay awake for the rest of the day.

'Mine's coffee, NATO, while you're there,' her mentor called after her.

*****

By Wednesday lunchtime, Mouse felt she knew enough about Hong Kong to answer specialist questions on Mastermind or to give a lecture. She already knew it was an amazing place but hadn't known the full history from the UK point of view.

When reading the documents, she discovered that Hong Kong had been a British colony from 1841 to present, except when it was occupied by the Japanese during most of the Second World War. There was a sidenote advising readers to use the word *Territory* instead of *Colony*, which was considered old-fashioned and harked back to the days of the British Empire. Mouse wasn't surprised to read that the UK became involved due to the opium wars where Hong Kong had been the key area for smuggling drugs into China, where it was prohibited. She was surprised to learn that only the New Territories and outlying islands were leased to the UK for ninety-nine years and that the UK had agreed to return the whole area to China. As Mouse read on, it actually made sense

75

– due to the scarcity of natural resources on Hong Kong Island and Kowloon, it seemed that China would only have to turn off the water supply to these areas and chaos would ensue! So the UK Government had agreed to hand over Hong Kong when the clock struck midnight at the start of 1 July 1997. As far as she was aware, the main aim between now and then was working towards a peaceful withdrawal and a fair deal for the locals.

She had also read about Headquarters British Forces Hong Kong. The Intelligence Services were housed on the 10th floor, the Command Group J1 and J3 on the 11th, the rest of the J Branches on the 12th floor and various other departments on the 13th and 14th. The 14th was also the home of the NAAFI, run by a friendly local known as Mr Lau, who was keen on teaching Cantonese to anyone he served. Most of his customers took his suggestions with good grace but Mouse had already witnessed a few warrant officers and middle-grade officers being short or rude to him. The man would look genuinely upset and she felt sorry for him. He was charming and likeable, unlike Mr Fong, the head barman in the Warrant Officers and Sergeants Mess. Mr Fong reminded her of the rude waiters in Wong Kei's in London's Soho and she intended to avoid him just as she had regarding visits to that infamous restaurant.

By the time Thursday arrived, Mouse was ready to meet the brigadier, confident that she'd be able to manage fairly well under Beth's tutelage. She was still nervous a few minutes prior to his arrival, for reasons having nothing to do with her work.

The corridor doors were open, and they could hear the lift ping every time someone arrived. People didn't wander onto this floor without reason, and this time, she just knew it was her new boss.

'Ah, Sergeant Halfpenny,' he said as he entered the office.

Mouse stood up at her desk. 'Good morning, Sir.'

'Good morning. Do come in,' he said, as if inviting her into his home.

She followed him and stood in front of the desk as he walked around it and sat down.

'Welcome to Hong Kong, Sergeant Halfpenny. A new start for you and for me with a new PA. Let's shake on new starts for us both.'

'Yes, Sir,' she said with a smile as they shook hands.

'Mine's a coffee, please, black with one. Grab yourself a drink too and bring in your notepad, then we'll get down to business.'

'That was a weird introduction.' Beth said to her as they were both getting brews for their bosses. 'As if you had some history?'

'We met in London like I already told you, Beth. It's the truth,' she added after seeing the sceptical look on Beth's face. That was all she needed, for her new workmate to start a rumour about an imagined relationship with the brigadier.

'There's been nobody since Guy died and it's up to you whether you want to believe me or put me into the same bracket as my predecessor.'

'Of course I believe you.' Beth looked crestfallen. 'But you have to admit it was a rather unusual introduction and I think you're hiding something.'

Mouse was a split second away from spilling the beans, but remembered she hardly knew this woman. She trusted her gut. 'Like I already said, there's nothing going on. He's a friend of Brigadier Riley who I worked for in London and we already know each other and that's the only history we have.'

'Fair enough,' Beth replied. 'I must get on. You know where I am if you need me.' She was all business now, knowing she wasn't getting anything juicy from Mouse, and that's the way the remainder of the day passed.

Friday was different. The offices had been a sea of calm from Monday to Thursday, but the general's MA returned on Friday in preparation for the general's return to office the following week. He went into the brigadier's office and the door was closed.

Ten minutes later the MA exited, then the brigadier called her in. 'I've told the MA you'll help him today, Sergeant Halfpenny.'

'Yes, Sir.'

'But first, a couple of things from me.'

She sat down with pen poised ready to take notes.

'Set up an appointment for Chief J3 to come and see me first thing Monday morning. Then SO1 J4 next, followed by Colonel Simms. Tell Colonel Simms I want to talk to him about the golf competition next month.'

'Yes, Sir.'

'Mrs Harding-Brown wants a dinner party next Saturday. You'll have been told the procedure?'

'Yes, Sir.'

'Invite Michael Yang and his wife, the Leveretts and the Campbells. I'll let you know who else to invite on Monday, after I've spoken to my wife. Anything for me?'

'Dinner party, seven for seven thirty, Sir? And what's the dress?'

'Yup, seven for seven thirty, and they'll know what to wear, thanks, Mouse.' It was the first time he'd called her by her nickname. It was quite common for senior officers to call their female NCOs by their first names and Beth already told her the general called her by her first name. Mouse used to get her knickers in a twist over such things, but now she was older and wiser, had no intention of making an issue of it. She had the posting she wanted and although events with her brother's family had put a dampener on it, she still intended to make the most of her time in Hong Kong. *Fresh start and all that*, she thought to herself.

The brigadier gathered up a few documents from his desk and put them into his briefcase.

'Enjoy your weekend, Mouse. Hong Kong is a fabulous place and I hope you make the most of your tour here.'

'I certainly plan on doing so, Sir. You have a good weekend too.' *We're almost besties now*, she giggled to herself as she gathered up his coffee mug and returned to her desk shortly after he left.

Major Sparks, the MA, looked up from the mountain of papers on his desk.

'I'm your line manager although you work for the brigadier.' he said. 'We'll have a chat when it's a bit quieter.'

'Nice to meet you, Sir.' Mouse went to his desk and they shook hands.

'Let Beth know when you're ready to give us a hand.'

She said she would and got straight to work on the tasks the brigadier had given her.

All that day it was as if someone had thrown a grenade in and they were dealing with the fallout. A number of people visited the MA, the phones were ringing off their hooks and it was all hands to the deck. Mouse was roped in to take messages, having to assess which were urgent and those that were routine and could wait. Of course, every caller thought their business was the most important. As far as she was concerned it was routine stuff and she knew she was being tested on her abilities to ensure some of the more senior officers were fobbed off in such a way so as to not feel put out. This would make them less likely to have a go at the MA when the general was about. She was familiar with some of the workings of outer offices due to her short stint at the MOD and was grateful for it. But Mouse knew she was a small fish in this big pond and vowed to have a good time in Hong Kong, both on and off duty, without drawing undue attention to herself.

She should have known herself better by now.

Chapter 5 – Before They Go

There were three weeks before Graham, Grace and Elfie left; Mouse and Graham's family had vowed to make the most of their time together, not knowing when they would next see each other.

Some days, Grace was able to meet Mouse after work and go shopping or meet up for dinner - and what shopping! Mouse had never known any place like it. From Temple Street Market where you could buy literally anything as cheap as chips, to the upmarket malls where designer goods were readily available, to the streets of Kowloon where every electronic gadget was available at the right price. Mouse was awestruck. There were preferred jewellers that visited the married quarters that the singlies were put in touch with. Military personnel were in receipt of an extra overseas allowance whilst serving abroad so had extra disposable income. She had to temper her excitement with the fact that Grace could tire easily and knew she wouldn't be able to fully explore what was available until she was on her own.

She'd been informed about the shopping before arrival, but it had still been beyond her wildest dreams. What nobody had told her about was the smell. Bean curd was the most horrendous smell that Mouse had ever encountered. It was almost tangible, and she could smell the stuff from two hundred metres. It was even worse than the unwanted meat chucked out with the rubbish and left to rot in the heat of the day.

On this particular Saturday, the plan was for Mouse to buy a new digital camera. Grace was accompanying her to Kowloon while Graham took Elfie swimming. It was the family's last Saturday in Hong Kong and they were handing over their quarter the following Monday and moving into the Airport Hotel. As a very special treat, they planned to meet up at the Furama Hotel's revolving restaurant for a meal later that day.

At the Star Ferry terminal, the women paid their dollar for the more expensive upstairs and joined the queue.

It wasn't overly busy and they got on the ferry and leaned over the railings, taking in the view of Kowloon, on the other side.

'It still amazes me that you get all this for one Hong Kong dollar,' said Grace. 'I'll never tire of this amazing place and will miss it so much.'

'And I'll miss you guys. It's so unfair.'

'We'll miss you too. And you're right, life is unfair, but we just have to play the cards we're dealt, Mouse. What other choice do we have?'

Grace was right as usual and although Mouse was sad, it would have been selfish to dwell on it and spoil the little time they had left together. They should make the most of their last shopping trip, but she'd need to ensure she didn't wear Grace out. Tonight's dinner was going to be special and Mouse was determined that Grace would be there with Graham and Elfie. Unbeknown to her, Grace had vowed that she was going to make it for her second and last visit to the Furama's revolving restaurant and when she'd made up her mind about something, there was no stopping her.

They both felt invigorated when standing outside on the ferry, waiting for it to stop and for the workers to quickly secure it and put the plank down. Within seconds they were surrounded by locals – Hong Kongers didn't queue, and people pushed past them to hurry to their next destinations, some treating them as if they were invisible.

'For pity's sake!' Mouse hated bad manners and as much as she tried not to let it bother her, she still allowed herself to be wound up.

'Sorry.' One woman bumped into her and had the grace to look genuinely apologetic.

'She probably thought you were going to get a knife out and stab her by the look on your face,' Grace said, trying her best to keep her own straight.

'It's okay, love.' Mouse shouted after her, but the woman was long gone.

'I'll try harder, Grace. I'll drive myself nuts if I don't.'

Her sister in law laughed and linked her arm. But shortly after they unlinked. It was too difficult trying to keep hold of each other and having to weave in and out of the crowds. Grace turned left, and Mouse thought she was going the wrong way. She said nothing, not trusting her own sense of direction that had let her down so many times before. There were less glitzy looking shops this way and more street food vendors and little markets. They walked for a few minutes in silence until Grace stopped when she saw a small number of people crowded around a man.

'Excuse me,' Grace said politely and a few of the locals smiled and let them through so they could see what was going on. One man held a live snake while another spoke to the crowd. Both men looked up and down the street, and when they were satisfied that they could carry on unhindered, the man not holding the snake said something in Cantonese and some of the onlookers gave him some money; Grace was one of them.

Mouse had no idea what was going on but put some space between herself and the man holding the snake. She needn't have worried as the poor reptile wasn't long for this world.

'Brace yourself,' said Grace as the man holding the snake drew a knife from his pocket. He nodded to the crowd, took a theatrical deep breath then plunged the knife into the poor snake and kept cutting halfway down its body. The snake writhed to no avail. The other man produced what looked like some sort of measuring jug and collected some of the snake's bodily fluid.

Mouse put a hand over her mouth, trying her best not to heave. When she was sure she'd composed herself, she spoke. 'Why the hell have you brought me here, Grace?'

'Shh, it'll become clear. And that's not the worst of it.'

When it was apparent no more juices were coming out of the snake, the man decanted the liquid into cups or vials. The man holding the now dead snake dumped it in a bin then took one of the cups from his assistant. He gave it to one of the women who had paid the money.

'Oh my God, no,' said Mouse, anticipating what was going to happen.

'It's the juices from the gall bladder and it's supposed to be a cure all,' said Grace. 'And I'm willing to try anything once.'

'Oh no, Grace. That's disgusting you can't. And that poor animal…'

Mouse was shocked into silence as she watched one of the women in the crowd neck the contents.

'I think I'm going to throw up…'

'Get a grip, Mouse. I do feel guilty about the snake and I agree it's quite disgusting, but western medicine can't cure me so I'm seriously thinking about giving this a try.'

'But Grace…'

'What would you do in my situation?'

'I certainly wouldn't be drinking a snake's insides, that's for sure.'

'It's the juices from the gall bladder. According to ancient Chinese medicine it can help with all sorts of ills and apparently, can't do me any harm.'

'Aye, and tiger penis is supposed to be an aphrodisiac. Would you take that too?'

'Tigers are an endangered species, Mouse. Snakes aren't.'

'And the gall bladder. Isn't that where all the waste from the animal goes?' Mouse had no idea whether this was true. She was just worried for Grace and would do anything to put her off.

'Don't you think I've done my research? Snake bile is used to cure a number of illnesses, like I said.'

'You're really serious about this aren't you?' Mouse interrupted

'I don't know how long I'll be here, Mouse, because of this illness. But I'm willing to give anything a try if there's a chance I can prolong my time with Graham and Elfie.'

Mouse heard the desperation in her voice and realised this wasn't an argument she was going to win. She gave Grace a sad smile and they hugged. As she broke the hug, she caught a glimpse of one of the Gurkha soldiers she'd seen in the office, together with a young Chinese NCO who she'd seen in the lift in HMS Tamar. The first thing that had struck her about the Chinese NCO was his uncanny resemblance to Chinese Pete, the waiter she had found dead in the Sergeants Mess in Rheindahlen. This was unusual as, in her limited experience, the local soldiers and Gurkhas did not mix. Perhaps there were exceptions to the rule. She noticed the Chinese corporal had another sticking plaster on his wrist and wondered what the injury was as he had been wearing one the last time she saw him.

'I'm sorry, Grace. It's just that it looks pretty disgusting and is there actually any medical evidence to suggest it works?' Mouse returned to the present.

'You're right. But loads of people use different medicines when Western stuff doesn't do the job. I'm not saying it'll work but if I don't give it a try I'll never know. Oh, and I've been taking it without knowing by the way.'

'You what?'

'Our lovely amah thought it might do me good, so she's been making me herbal tea and putting it in there.'

'Ack-O?'

Grace nodded.

'But couldn't you taste something horrible?'

'This tea is made with some sort of exotic mushroom that's supposed to boost your immune system and tastes pretty horrible anyway, so it didn't make much difference. I only found out when I made a cup for myself and it didn't taste quite the same. I had a conversation with Ack-O and her niece. One of the other amahs made her come clean. Poor woman thought we were going to sack her.'

'So you being you, decided to come and see for yourself. Is that about right.'

Grace chuckled. 'You know me so well.'

'Well, good luck with it. I hope it works.'

'I won't be able to get it back home, Mouse. But I will be able to get the mushrooms. I might have to travel to find a shop that stocks them, but I do believe the tea makes me feel better.'

If it worked for Grace, or Grace thought it worked for her, Mouse mentally corrected herself, she would say no more. Grace took the liquid and put it into a sealed jar she'd brought with her. She wrapped the jar in a carrier bag and put that into her handbag

'Shall we go and get you a camera now?' Mouse agreed and they turned around and headed back towards the shops that sold any shiny gadget or latest state of the art electronic equipment, that money could buy.

*****

The shopping finished for the day, Mouse and Grace hurried to the Star Ferry for the return journey. They were both looking forward to meeting Graham and Elfie at the edge of the Wanchai District, for the buffet lunch at La Ronda revolving restaurant in the Furama Hotel. Mouse wasn't used to eating at posh hotels and was excited at the prospect. Looking at the hotel from a distance, it was like somebody had put a disk on the top. They got in the lift and pressed the button for the 30th floor. There was a small queue and Mouse switched off to Elfie's chatter as she peeked inside. Tables moved slowly giving the clientele ample opportunity to take in the stunning views of Hong Kong island, from the Wanchai District, to the harbour on the other side. As they were shown to their table, Mouse noticed the tourists savouring the views, whereas the locals seemed to ignore the views and savoured their food. One such person had a plate filled with oysters and was nosily picking up each one and eating, as if somebody would take away the plate before he had a chance to finish. Another picked up a whole fried egg between his chopsticks and nosily chomped away.

'Look at that man,' Elfie said, and a number of people turned to stare. The man was totally oblivious though and carried on chewing his food with his mouth wide open. Mouse had long since realised that having money didn't equate to having class, or indeed, manners. She shot him her best *you disgusting pig* look which the man ignored.

It was all an assault on the senses. The fabulous view with the high-rise buildings, the South China Sea, dappled

85

with ferries and assorted junks, and the streets below where people went about their business, like little ants on their own missions. Then there was the buffet. An expanse of shapes and colours in the form of seafood – some of which Mouse had never seen or heard of, the same with the salads and meats which included both hot and cold. Her nose and eyes fought for attention and that was before she saw the selection of desserts.

'Good grief. Where do I even begin?' Mouse asked, standing and holding her plate, too dumbstruck to start making choices.

'Dunno, but you'd better move before you get knocked over,' said Grace, as people tutted at her sister-in-law when they were forced to walk around her to get their food.

'Come on, Auntie Mouse, I'm hungry.'

That did the trick and she started piling a selection of salads onto her plate.

'It's all you can eat, Miss,' said a woman who was replenishing the crab salad. 'You can always come back for more.'

Mouse thanked her and returned to the table.

Once they were all seated the adults enjoyed their food while Elfie picked at hers and chatted away, before announcing. 'I want to go the toilet, Mummy.' A knowing look passed between her parents.

'Elfie likes to check out the toilets in every hotel or restaurant we visit. Don't you, darling?' said Graham.

'That's because I need a wee, Daddy.'

Graham said he'd take her, but Grace was having none of it. 'I'll go, Graham, it's fine.'

'She thinks every time I offer to help it's because she's ill. But sometimes I'm just trying to be nice.' He sighed.

'It must be difficult. I know how strong-willed Grace can be. But why don't you speak to her about it?'

'Yeah, I'll do that,' Graham replied, both of them knowing that he wouldn't.

'It's not usual for Chinese and Gurkha soldiers to hang around together when they're off duty is it?'

Graham shook his head. 'What do you think?'

'Yeah, that's what I thought too. But when me and Grace were shopping this morning, I saw two soldiers I recognised. The Gurkha who works for the Gurkha Major and a Chinese NCO I saw in the lift last week.'

'And you remember the Chinese NCO?'

'Only because he's the spitting image of Chinese Pete, the waiter I found dead in the Mess in JHQ.'

'That is very unusual, Mouse. You're right. In my experience the Gurkha soldiers and the Chinese soldiers slag each other off and stay well away from each other. Where was this?'

Mouse explained what they were doing.

'Aah, so Grace did buy that disgusting stuff. She said she was going to, but I thought she was kidding. I should know better by now shouldn't I?'

Mouse thought she might have dropped Grace in it but stopped stressing when Graham started laughing. Then he turned serious. 'Everything she's already been through yet she's taking this new illness with a pinch of salt. Grace never ceases to amaze me, Mouse.'

'Me too. I don't know how she stays sane, never mind being so optimistic. She's definitely a glass- half-full person.'

'I can't imagine life without her. Whenever I think…'

'Well don't think it,' Mouse interrupted. 'Make every goddamn minute count because you just don't know how many you have left. Trust me. I know better than most.'

Graham put his hand on his sister's forearm, in a tender moment of sibling contact passing between them.

'Does it get easier?'

'The unbearable stabbing pain has now turned into a dull ache. It's always there but I've learned to live with it.'

'Time's a great healer and all that.'

'That's total bollocks, Graham.'

'Auntie Mouse said…' said Elfie, as she returned to the table with her mum.

'That's enough, Elfie!' Grace stopped her daughter before she could repeat the word. 'Auntie Mouse is very naughty.'

'I am and I'm sorry, Elfie. I won't do it again.'

The little girl looked satisfied and they carried on with their meal. After the initial oohs and aahs when choosing their desserts, even Elfie was quiet as she satisfied her sweet tooth.

'Would you like to go to the petting zoo later, Elfie? Just you and me.' asked Mouse and Elfie was full of chatter again, telling the adults how much she enjoyed it there.

'Thanks,' Grace mouthed, giving Mouse a grateful look and looking forward to spending some time alone later in the day with Graham, which was a rarity these days.

Sunday was quieter and she again joined her family for a sumptuous fish and chip lunch in the Connaught Centre, accompanied by a bottle of their house champagne.

'Just because we can,' Graham said, before they said their goodbyes and Mouse returned to the Mess to get everything ready for the work week.

Mouse rushed through her work until Thursday. Aside from her cock-up in inviting the wrong Michael Yang to the brigadier's dinner party, her week was going well so far. The boss took it with good grace.

'I know, Mouse, we'll have a Yang party. Get me the card index and I'll tell you which ones to invite?'

'Okay, Sir, but won't they be offended?'

'Offended? Certainly not. They'll be most delighted to have received an invitation to dine with the Deputy Commander and his lovely wife and will name drop the fact at parties for the foreseeable.'

The brigadier could be amusing, and Mouse was starting to like him, despite his alley cat morals.

On her way to take some papers to Chief J3 before knocking off work early, Mouse noticed the Gurkha Major approach the general's office. Thinking nothing of it she packed up and rushed to the lift. The Gurkha corporal, together with Chinese Pete's lookalike were already in the lift. Unsure whether it was her over-active imagination or not, it seemed to Mouse as if the men were purposely acting as if they didn't know each other. There was definitely something going on there and Mouse knew she wouldn't be happy until she discovered what it was. But that would have to wait. She needed to get to her room, change as quickly as she could and get to the airport hotel to spend the evening with Graham, Grace and Elfie before they left Hong Kong for good. Distracted, she travelled down to the ground floor then made a play of approaching the security guard as if she had business with him. She watched as the corporals left the building. The Gurkha looked back at the building before walking off in the opposite direction to the Chinese NCO. *Curious,* thought Mouse, before the security guard's voice broke her train of thought.

'Did you want something, Mouse?' he asked in his Northern Scottish accent.

'No thanks, Bill. I'd forget my head if it wasn't screwed on,' she replied as she made her way back to the lift. Bill rolled his eyes at her back then carried on with his crossword puzzle.

Showered, changed and ready to go, Soo Key was waiting in the lobby of HMS Tamar when Mouse arrived thirty minutes later. He'd offered to drop her off at the airport as he wanted to say goodbye to Graham and his family too.

'I'll pick you up later, too,' Soo Key had offered but Mouse declined.

'It's fine, Soo Key. I'll make my own way back but thanks for the offer.' The man had little spare time due to his busy job and Mouse had no intention of prevailing on his good nature.

She braced herself as they parked up and made their way to the airport hotel. It was going to be emotional, but she knew she'd have to keep a grip on her emotions so as not to upset Elfie.

The Airport Hotel was an integral part of the airport infrastructure and it was less than a five- minute walk from there to the terminal for their flight back to London. Mouse had been there earlier in the week so knew exactly where to go, but Graham and his family weren't in their room. Soo Key followed her to the lounge area where Graham was reading, Grace was doing a puzzle and Elfie was putting the final touches to Mickey Mouse and Pluto in her drawing book. Her tongue was lolling from one side of her mouth like it did when she was concentrating. Mouse stopped dead and put a finger to her lips, so Soo Key didn't move an inch further. She wanted to memorise this image of the people she loved so she could recall it during any sad or difficult times. The spell was broken when Grace looked up.

'Look who's here!' she said to Elfie, who threw her pen down and ran to Mouse. She wrapped her arms around her auntie's legs.

'Don't let them take me, Auntie Mouse, I don't want to go,' she said, before bursting into tears. Other people in the lounge looked on with interest and Elfie soon sensed she had an audience. 'I… want…to…stay…with…you,' she said, in between sobs.

'Show Auntie Mouse your drawing, Elfie,' said Graham. His daughter hesitated for a moment to give it a bit of thought but then changed her mind. She loosened herself from her auntie's legs and decided to address the audience at large.

'They're making me go to England,' she said to the room in general. 'Where it's cold and rains all the time and the shops close early.'

A number of people laughed which did not amuse Elfie. 'It's not funny. I won't see my Auntie Mouse for ages.'

'You can visit me, Elfie,' said Mouse. 'And I'll come and visit you whenever I'm home.'

'Okay. Come and see my drawing.' The hysterics over not long after they began, Elfie held her auntie's hand and pulled her impatiently to where her parents were sitting.

Soo Key and Graham chatted for a bit while the women indulged Elfie. The time flew and it was bittersweet for Mouse, knowing that moving near her parents was the right decision for Grace, but also knowing she would miss them so much. She wouldn't have pushed for a posting to

Hong Kong if she'd known they were going to leave so soon after her arrival. Saying that, Mouse admitted to herself that she was glad to be there and if anything could help her move on with her life, then this was the place to do it.

Soo Key left soon afterwards and the hours then flew by. Despite her best efforts trying to fight sleep, Elfie nodded off. Having already checked their luggage in via the hotel's complimentary service and with boarding passes issued, Graham and Grace were able to leave it until the last moment before leaving for the gate.

They hugged and Mouse did her best to hold back her tears.

'Don't get involved in whatever you were thinking about that Gurkha and Chinese soldier,' Graham said to his sister.

Mouse gave him an *as if I would* look, but they both knew he was wasting his time and if she had an itch, she would go ahead and scratch it.

'Take care of yourself, Grace, and don't overdo it.'

Grace simply nodded and gave Mouse another hug.

Graham was carrying Elfie who opened her eyes and yawned.

'We're going on the plane now,' said Graham.

'Bye, bye, Auntie Mouse. I love you.'

'I love you too, sweetheart. Bye bye.' Mouse turned and walked away so they wouldn't see her tears. She turned after a while and her family waved to her. She blew them a kiss, then they disappeared out of sight. Wiping her eyes, she gave a sigh and did her best to compose herself before making her way to the MTR, to catch the underground train and return to the Mess.

Beth left the following week and, having not socialised with any of the people she'd met in the Mess, Mouse felt more alone than she had in ages.

She needed to find something to occupy her brain outside of work and had no idea of the danger she was about to put herself in.

Chapter 6 – Alone in a city of five million people

Mouse knew there was no chance of her being promoted into Beth's job; there was no handover and a week after Beth left, her replacement, Hazel, arrived. She was married to a civilian and it amazed Mouse to discover that some thought Hazel and her husband weird because she was serving, and he was a civvy. This was the nineteen eighties for God's sake, and women who did things differently were still thought of as strange. While they got on well enough, there was no instant spark of friendship and had they not worked together, they would not have been friends.

The Sergeants Mess was mixed, and Mouse kept herself to herself. She thought some of the other groups of senior NCOs to be cliquey, many thought she was aloof. Unbeknown to Mouse, she was labelled as *stuck up,* and someone who thought she was something special because she worked for senior officers. As she chose not to socialise with Hazel during her down time, she became pretty much a loner.

Mouse was happy to explore on her own and it gave her the freedom to go where she wanted and when, without being judged.

One morning before work, Mouse had decided to go for a swim. She hadn't gone to her aerobics classes the previous week, and was feeling sluggish. They were lucky in that there was a pool for military personnel just outside HMS Tamar building, within the compound. After a thirty-minute session she felt invigorated and headed back to the building to shower and change prior to going to work, and was surprised too see a familiar face at the security desk as she entered the building.

'Hello, Sir.'

'Well, if it isn't Sergeant Halfpenny.'

She shook hands with Guy's previous and last RSM.

'I was going to look you up and suggest we go for a drink while I'm visiting - now you've saved me a job.'

'That would be great, Sir.' Mouse was genuinely pleased to see him and hoped he would have the time to go out to dinner so she could speak to him about the Chinese NCO.

'This is Major Frewings, Sergeant Halpfenny, OC 158 Company.'

'Hello, Sir, nice to meet you.' said Mouse, holding out her hand. The major gave it a quick shake.

'Sergeant Halfpenny works for…'

'Come on, RSM. We have work to do,' Major Frewings interrupted.

Charming, she thought as the RSM threw him a dirty look, and Mouse had no doubt he would speak to him about his rudeness later. It would have been bad etiquette to do it in front of her.

'We'll see you later, Sergeant Halfpenny,' the RSM said, before turning and giving his full attention to the security guard.

She entered the lift wondering why he was visiting and went to get ready for work.

Later that morning, the brigadier came out of the general's office and, as he was passing her desk, he curled a finger and beckoned Mouse to follow him into his office.

'Reschedule my appointments for the rest of the day, Mouse, please. OC 158 is coming to see me at eleven o'clock with a visiting SIB RSM. Get SO2 Sneaky-Beaky to come to the meeting too, and I don't want to be disturbed.'

'Ooh, that sounds interesting,' she said, fishing for information. Sometimes the brigadier humoured her and gave her some juicy tidbits, but not today.

'Just get it sorted.'

'Yes, Sir.

Mouse readied the brew kit in time for their appointment. Quite often, when officers and warrant officers had a call with the boss, the officers were called in first and the warrant officers had to wait outside in the lobby until the boss was ready to discuss the issue at their level. She hoped this would be the case today when she would be able to sit outside with Guy's old RSM, tell him about the NCO who was the spitting image of Chinese Pete, and also explain why she thought something fishy was going on.

It wasn't to be.

All three arrived together and the brigadier's door was closed. Before she had a chance to knock on it to take them through and introduce the RSM, the boss opened it.

The RSM was introduced to him and hands were shaken, then all three followed the brigadier back into his office.

'Give us ten minutes, then bring in some coffee please, Sergeant Halfpenny.'

'Yes, Sir.' It must be a pretty formal meeting, she thought, if he was calling her by her rank. But not to worry, she would see the RSM later and explain her worries. Failing that, he wanted to meet up for a drink, so she'd find out where he was staying in the Mess and make the arrangements.

She couldn't even get the gist of what they were discussing when she took in a pot of coffee and some biscuits, because they became silent as soon as she opened the door. The brigadier started talking about how he'd won some cash on the horses at the Happy Valley race track. It was no good trying to have a sneaky listen by the door as the general and his staff were in, so she went about her daily business, albeit distracted by thoughts of people up to no good.

Just when Mouse thought she'd burst if she didn't go to the loo, they came out. It was twelve forty-five. Before she had a chance to make any arrangements with the RSM, the brigadier called her into the office. The RSM gestured goodbye with a hand and off she went into the office.

'Close the door behind you,' he said, 'and you won't need your notebook.'

The brigadier sounded so serious that Mouse expected a bollocking and didn't take a seat as she usually would. She wracked her brain, wondering what she'd done wrong.

'That meeting was highly classified and didn't happen. Do you understand?'

'Yes, Sir.'

'The SIB and sneaky-beakys are carrying out an investigation, and for now, it's undercover. Nobody knows the RSM is here and I want it to stay that way.'

'But, Sir he signed in, and if he's staying in the Mess…'

'He's not staying in the Mess, Mouse, and he signed in under a pseudonym. I'm telling you this because I know you know each other and that you were going to meet. Without wanting to over dramatize the situation or sound like an MI6 agent, you must not give away his cover or discuss that meeting or this visit with anyone. Do you understand?'

'Yes, Sir. But you may want…'

'That's it for now, thanks. I'm off for a long lunch and will be back about three. Don't book any appointments for this afternoon.'

'Yes, Sir,' she said, and then left the office. She was sure this was something to do with the death of Chinese Pete in Germany, and had an inkling that the two NCOs she'd seen fraternising were definitely up to something. *Would it be a stretch to imagine the two were connected?* wondered Mouse. Especially as the Chinese soldier had to be related to the waiter, Chinese Pete. She knew all the jokes about Chinese people looking like each other, but aside for hair and eye colour, it was a load of old rot. Perhaps the Chinese NCO was out for revenge after the murder of a member of his family? Or perhaps he was part of a triad criminal gang and Chinese Pete had been involved in that. She drove herself nuts for the rest of the day with her 'maybe this' and maybe thats'. After spending several hours wracking her brains, Mouse had to admit no idea where to start she and decided it would be best to sleep on it and let her subconscious do the workings out for her.

By Friday, she was none the wiser and the weekend loomed. She had received an invitation to go to Sunday lunch from Hazel, who was going along with her husband and some of their friends, and was looking forward to that, but Saturday was a day to be spent alone. Mouse thought she'd make the most of it, got herself a map and some leaflets, and decided to become a tourist.

It was monsoon season and was raining heavily outside, but the forecast was for gaps in the rain later that day. So Mouse started her day indoors. After wandering around Pacific Place for a while, she decided she wasn't in the mood for shopping for designer gear, so when the rain eased off a bit, she took the Star Ferry to Kowloon where she walked around Temple Street Market for a while, still in awe at the variety of both goods and people in the place. Hong Kong was a little like the bar in one of the Star Wars movies where peoples of every race could be found, and Temple Street Market seemed to be the centre of diversity.

After buying t-shirts and shorts that she didn't need, and a lightweight waterproof hoody that she did, Mouse checked out the touristy items. There was a massive range of ornaments, clothes of all assortments and every make of copy watch. She must have looked like a tourist as the eyes of vendors lit up when they saw her and they shouted prices at her as she walked by, believing that if she stopped to look, they'd get a sale.

'Copy watch, Missy,' said one. 'Like real Gucci.'

Mouse stopped to look at that one. The colour of the strap matched that of the WRAC stable belt, and she'd noticed Beth wearing one with her summer dress. It looked smart so she decided to go for it. A few minutes and thirty-five dollars later she'd had enough.

Mouse contemplated going to one of the posh hotels for afternoon tea – the Peninsula being the epitome of posh in her eyes – but it was far too early. Without realising what she was doing, Mouse found herself heading towards the area where Grace had bought the disgusting snake medicine. Once she found herself recognising where she was, her sixth sense kicked in and she began to properly look around. Her heart hammered in her chest when she saw a Gurkha soldier and instantly recognised him as the junior NCO she'd seen with Chinese Pete's lookalike. He could have been out for a bit of shopping or on family business, but instinct told Mouse to follow him. She almost lost sight of him on the MTR but by keeping a discreet distance, she kept him in her sights, wondering if he was headed for Kai Tak Airport.

He wasn't.

The Gurkha veered off before then and Mouse had an inkling where he was going. The infamous Walled City was a den of iniquity for drugs, prostitution, money laundering and any other criminal activity one could imagine. She'd heard it was controlled by triads and the area was out of bounds to military personnel, their dependants and anyone in Hong Kong working with the British Forces. She had to make a decision. Her heart started to beat faster and she felt a tingle of excitement rush through her veins. *Try not to ponder the worst possible outcome*, she thought, as she followed him into the unknown.

The rain was back, so Mouse tied back her hair and put up her hood, covering it. She was taller than most Chinese people but didn't look out of place from the back and, as far as she could see, most people were hurrying about, minding their own business. As well as trying to follow without being seen, Mouse was also concentrating on avoiding umbrella spokes, the majority of which seemed to be at her eye height.

Within seconds of entering the out of bounds area, the heavens opened, and even those with umbrellas or raincoats started running for cover. Before she knew it, there was hardly anyone on the streets and Mouse now felt that she stood out like a sore thumb. She had lost sight of the Gurkha soldier who must have ducked into one of the buildings, but she had no idea which one. *The best laid plans and all that*, she thought, as she tried to remember the way out. She kept moving, not wanting to look even more conspicuous, and tried to stay under awnings where possible. She was lost within a few minutes and felt panic rising inside her. She heard a woman calling in Chinese and looked about her. The old woman was serving noodles from a stall behind which was a building where a number of locals were sitting and eating. She beckoned to Mouse. The people eating inside looked dry so Mouse jogged the short distance. When out of the wet, she shook herself dry like a dog coming in from the rain. The old woman laughed and made a big deal of showing Mouse to a small table inside. Mouse was grateful that the other customers ignored her, either too busy eating their food or preferring to ignore what was going on. The woman gave her a piece of tatty card that showed pictures of bowls of food, accompanied by Chinese writing. Mouse studied the card. The woman folded her arms and tapped her foot before turning her head and shouting. Another woman appeared who Mouse thought was probably from the Phillipines or Thailand. The Chinese woman said something to her and the younger assistant smiled at Mouse.

'Noodles or rice, Missy, and spicy or mild?' Mouse was grateful that her English was perfect.

'Spicy noodles would be lovely thank you and… a can of coke if you have one?'

'Coke. Certainly.' She said something in Chinese to the older woman and they both laughed hysterically.

'Coke if we have one,' repeated the assistant, now chuckling to herself. 'Missy, we sell everything,' she said, before disappearing in the direction of the enticing aroma.

The food was delicious, and Mouse tried not to think of the conditions in the kitchen, if, indeed, this place had one. She asked for directions to the nearest MTR as she paid.

'I think I've taken a wrong turning,' she said to the younger woman.

Mouse was surprised when the woman disappeared and returned with a pen and piece of paper. She drew a rough outline of where they were now and gave Mouse directions as she drew the best way to exit the area. She marked two crosses on the paper. 'Don't go here, or here,' she said. 'This is a dangerous place with some bad people, but if you stick to these directions, you'll be fine.'

'The food was delicious, thanks, and thanks for your help too. I hope to see you again.'

'My pleasure, Missy. If you take a wrong turning this way in future, make sure someone comes with you.' she smiled.

Mouse didn't expect to meet the friendly assistant again, but she was in for a surprise.

*****

It was still wet on Sunday but extremely humid so was too hot for jeans. Mouse wore a pair of patterned lightweight trousers and a plain purple top for the lunch. Checking herself in the mirror, she added a heavy necklace and dangling, three-colour-gold earrings – one of the last presents Guy had bought for her. After a moment of reflection, she gave herself a mental shake and a final once over, now satisfied that her outfit was smart enough for the occasion, but not too over the top.

As she walked into the Marriot Hotel in Pacific Place, Mouse was directed to the restaurant. She could see straight away that it was another buffet lunch set-up and looked forward to getting stuck in a little later. Looking around, she saw Hazel sitting at a long table, next to a man who looked considerably older than her. Neil Mitchum was also there, along with a number of other people Mouse didn't recognise and she couldn't see the faces of the people sitting opposite Hazel and Neil.

'Here she is,' said Hazel, as she saw Mouse approach. Then she added, 'Everyone this is Mouse,' as Mouse arrived at the table. Individual introductions were made. The older man was Hazel's husband George, and after a quick hello and a few niceties, Mouse tried to hide her surprise when she looked at Neil's wife.

'This is Alice,' Neil said. 'We've saved you a seat there.'

'Hello, Alice.'

'Nice to meet you, Mouse,' she replied. 'Neil's told me all about you.'

Has he indeed, Mouse thought as she took her seat next to Alice, who looked a lot nicer in her smart clothes than she had when she had served Mouse the food then drawn her a map the day before.

The others at the table were a male and female Military Police couple, and a British civilian Hong Kong Policeman who sat on the other side of Mouse. They were all

99

coupled up and Mouse had the feeling they would try to set her up with Tony, the civvy cop who, she had noticed, was very good-looking.

'How long have you been in Hong Kong, Mouse?' he asked, and they got talking.

'I was seconded from the Met Police three years ago and decided to make my permanent home in Hong Kong. The offer was too good to refuse,' he said.

Mouse tried to concentrate on her starter, but she felt a spark when she spoke to the policeman sitting next to her, something she hadn't felt since Guy had died, and was struggling with how to deal with it. There was also the situation with Alice, and she wanted to speak to her in private as soon as she could.

'Excuse me for a few minutes,' said Alice after the starters had been cleared away and the smokers grabbed their packets and headed for the door.

'I'll come with you,' said Mouse and they both headed for the ladies' room.

Alice did a quick check and nobody else was there. 'I co-own our business,' she said. 'And need my independence so had no intention of giving it up.'

'What about…'

'Neil knows I work but he thinks it's at a restaurant in Kowloon.'

'He's bound to find out.'

'He won't. He loves me but has no interest in my work. Most people think I'm just his arm candy and we're both happy to let them think that's our arrangement.'

'Your arrangement?'

The door opened and neither felt comfortable carrying on their discussion when a woman neither knew entered. They smiled at the unknown woman while Mouse washed her hands and Alice looked in the mirror and adjusted her hair.

'Why don't we meet next week for a proper chat,' said Alice. 'After you finish work one evening?'

Mouse agreed. 'You know I can't come to…'

'Of course. Do you like curry?'

'I love curry.'

'We'll go to Sherry Punjab in Chung King Mansions.' Alice said, opening her purse and passing Mouse a card with details of the restaurant. Helpfully, the card had directions on the reverse. 'Tuesday all right?'

The brigadier was out of office Tuesday to Thursday, so a dinner date on Tuesday was fine.

'That's great,' said Mouse.

Although it wasn't discussed, both women knew it was in their best interests not to discuss Saturday's meeting in the Walled City with anyone else.

Mouse felt more relaxed when she returned to the table and decided to enjoy the company of Tony. There was an undeniable attraction and they chatted about her first impressions of Hong Kong and how she couldn't wait to explore the rest of it.

'You should let me show you around,' Tony said. 'I know some very interesting areas, off the beaten track.'

It surprised her, and her face must have reacted without her knowing.

'I'm sorry if that seems forward. Forget I said it,' he quickly added.

'No, it's not that...' Mouse took a deep breath deciding to bite the bullet. 'I think I'd like that, thanks,' she replied, and made a mental note to explain to Guy later on.

'Great. How about next weekend? My last shift is on Thursday night so I'm yours until Monday morning.'

'Err,' said Mouse as she realised the rest of the group had gone quiet and were watching them both.

'I think they're putting the main course out,' Hazel's husband George commented. 'Shall we have a look?'

Taking the hint, Neil nodded to Alice and followed her to the buffet. Hazel and George went next, followed by the others.

'Well that was a bit awkward,' said Tony. Mouse looked at him and they both burst out laughing. She took a swig of wine when she'd calmed down.

'Would you like to have dinner on Friday night, Mouse and let me show you around on Saturday?'

'I think I can manage that, Tony,'

'Great. Do you know the Bull and Bear in Hutchison House?'

'The Expat Place? My brother showed me that one. I think I can find my way there. Is that where we're going for dinner?'

'No. I thought we could meet there for a drink, then decide what we fancy to eat a bit later. What do you think?'

She liked the way he asked her opinion instead of organising everything or making assumptions that she'd be happy with his choices. 'Happy with that.'

'Does six o'clock suit you or is that too early?'

'That's fine. Talking of food, the main course smells yummy,' Mouse said, getting up. Tony followed her to the buffet.

The rest of the afternoon passed too quickly, and Mouse left the hotel's restaurant looking forward to both dinner with Alice on Tuesday and with Tony on Friday, but both for completely different reasons.

Mouse recce'd Chung King Mansions after work on Monday. Although she knew her way to places such as the Star Ferry, Nathan Road and the Central and some of the Mid-Level Districts, she still had lots of exploring to do and wasn't familiar with many places. Chung King Mansions was a microcosm, almost a village in itself by the looks of it. She noted the shopping areas were mainly on the ground floor and the accommodation on many of the other floors. Alice had told her that the *Sherry Punjab* Restaurant was on the third floor. As there were only three floors, she decided to take the stairs instead of the lift. Not her best decision. Halfway up the first set of stairs the stench hit her. Something was rotting and, prone to exaggeration, Mouse was convinced she'd find a body at the bend of the stairs. There was no body, but the first pile of rubbish consisted of what looked like rotten fruit. Some of it was moving. 'Urgh,' she said out loud and rushed up the next set of stairs. At every balcony there was rubbish – some was food waste, others were shoes, old clothes or broken furniture. The stairs were extremely grotty and looked like they hadn't been cleaned in centuries. Arriving on the third floor she saw a sign for the restaurant - it was just around the corner from the staircase and the sign. Mouse was pleased to see that the ornate door was clean, and she was able to peek through the small glass panel. About to turn and leave now that she knew she could find her way there, the door opened.

'Come in, come in,' said the Indian man.

'Thank you,' she replied and entered, not wanting to tell the man that she was only recce-ing the restaurant for another night. Now she would end up having curry on two consecutive nights.

'How many, Ma'am?'

'Just me, please.' He didn't blink an eyelid but led Mouse to a small table for two in an alcove where she could see other diners, but not all of them could see her. It was quite early, and the restaurant had yet to fill up. Mouse was surprised to see two Gurkha personnel enter with a Chinese man, and even more surprised when she recognised one of the Gurkhas as the NCO who worked for the Gurkha Major, and the soldier who was the lookalike of Chinese Pete. She didn't recognise the third and made a play of studying her menu. The men hadn't seen her. Alarm thrilled through her body as the Gurkha she recognised approached a table near her and almost sat down. The other, who Mouse noticed was dressed much smarter than the two she recognised, said something in Gurkhali, raising his voice and the soldier who was about to sit down stopped himself and headed towards a door that she hadn't noticed before. He opened it and let the other two men walk through first. He followed and closed the door behind him. By his bearing and authority, she assumed the unknown man was an officer – he didn't look mature enough to be a Gurkha SNCO. She had no idea who he was but wanted to find out. Her instinct told her something fishy was going on with those men and she was determined to get to the bottom of it.

A few minutes later a group of Chinese men walked in, each dressed in black suits, black ties and white shirts. The host who had directed Mouse to her table approached the men, clutching his hands as he did so and bowing slightly. He spoke in Chinese to the largest man while two of the others leaned against the wall with their arms folded. The group reminded Mouse of some Western men she'd seen strutting like peacocks in bars or nightclubs. This lot were something, or thought they were at the very least.

The host cowtowed as he led them to the private room that the others had entered. *Very interesting,* she thought. The bigger man reminded her of Earl for some reason and he looked familiar. She wondered why but nothing came immediately to mind except that she felt she'd seen him before. Mouse also wondered whether these men were the infamous triads that she'd heard mention of in London, Germany, and now Hong Kong.

As she finished her dinner Mouse, along with the other diners, looked up as they heard shouting coming from the private room. She recognised both Chinese and Gurkhali but had no idea of what was being said. The host wiped his brow with a handkerchief taken from his pocket and spoke to one of his staff who disappeared out of the door. A few minutes later six Indian-looking men arrived. One was the tallest person Mouse had ever seen and she stared as if rubbernecking a car crash. The man winked at her as he walked towards the door and she looked away.

A fleeting thought came that she should pay her bill and disappear, but it was only fleeting and she knew she was too intrinsically curious to leave before it got interesting. It didn't occur to her that she might become collateral damage if something did kick off.

Before the new arrivals entered the room, the door opened violently and one of the Chinese men in suits was thrown through. His tie was skew-whiff, there was blood on his face and his nose was bent at an awkward angle. The big Chinese man came out of the room next and the man with the broken nose bowed his head. The big man punched his subordinate in the stomach and the other man doubled over then fell to the floor. The big man kicked him once and shouted some abuse at him. He then walked back towards the door to the room. Before going in he shouted something and the man on the floor jumped up and followed. They went back into the room and the door closed behind them.

'What was all that about?' asked Mouse as she went to pay her bill.

'So sorry, Ma'am. Some men have business that's gone wrong.'

'So that's not a normal Monday night in your restaurant then?'

'No, Ma'am. You don't tell anyone please. It's bad for business.'

I bet it is, thought Mouse. 'I've heard good things about your restaurant and your food is delicious,' she said. 'I was going to bring a friend tomorrow night, but now…'

'I give you good discount,' he replied. 'See you tomorrow?'

'There won't be any fighting?'

'No, Ma'am. No fighting.'

'Very well then. We'll have the same table please, at seven o'clock.'

She left and on the journey back to the Mess, wondered how she could get to the bottom of whatever was going on.

Tuesday's dinner was eventful but for completely different reasons.

Mouse saw Alice's approach outside Chung King Mansions and called out to her. They greeted each other and Mouse felt like she was saying hello to an old friend. She wondered if Alice would become the closest she had to a friend in Hong Kong, and was looking forward to getting to know her, and especially interested in how she and Neil had got together.

'We'll take the lift,' Alice said. 'People use the stairwells as rubbish dumps, and it might put you off the restaurant which is clean with delicious food.'

Mouse didn't have a chance to respond as they entered the packed lift.

'Alice!' said the man who had greeted Mouse the night before. 'So good to see you and welcome back, Ma'am,' he added to Mouse.

Alice gave her a questioning look.

Deciding that honesty was the best policy, Mouse replied. 'I have a dreadful sense of direction and did a recce last night and ended up eating here.'

'Fair enough.' Alice gave a little laugh. 'We're none of us perfect are we?'

They were shown to the table Mouse had sat at the previous night and chatted while they studied the menu.

'So what made you ask for a posting to Hong Kong then, Mouse?'

'My husband was murdered a while ago and my brother and his family were based here. I needed a complete change of scenery so I can move on with my life.' She didn't generally share her feelings with many people, but Mouse felt she could talk to Alice and gut instinct made her trust her. She hoped her instincts were right.

'I'm so sorry to hear that. Sometimes words sound empty, but it must have been heart breaking.'

'That's an understatement and I was unhinged for such a long time. I'll always love Guy, but I'm beginning to think he would want me to get on with my life. The bastard who murdered him shot our dog at the same time.'

'Did they catch him? Is he in prison?'

'Oh, he was caught all right, but not by the police. He's rotting in hell, exactly as he should be.'

'I can't imagine what that must have been like.'

'My life was ruined, Alice, and I'll tell you the full story one day. But what about you? Why Hong Kong and how did you and Neil meet?'

Alice pondered for a moment, wondering how much to tell her new friend. Mouse had been honest with her so she decided to reciprocate, even though it would shock her and could possibly end the friendship before it began. Then again, she might find out from someone else anyway and that would make her lose trust, but most importantly, if she didn't want to be friends with her *warts and all,* thought Alice, she didn't deserve her friendship and they might as well stop it before they became any closer.

'In a knocking shop in the Walled City,' Alice said.

'Ha, ha,' Mouse replied, 'as if.' Then she looked at her new friend's face and saw the truth.

'I didn't mean…umm. What I meant was…'

'It's okay, Mouse, there's no need for you to be embarrassed.'

Mouse laughed nervously. 'So you're serious. Were you…umm-'

Now it was Alice's turn to laugh. 'Yes, I was one of the paid prostitutes. My family was given money and I was brought here from Thailand in exchange. I didn't have a choice, Mouse, but knowing that my family would have a better life made it bearable. The madame is a local and ensured we were treated well. After all, why would rich men want to pay for dirty or unclean girls. So except for the sex, life wasn't that bad.'

'Really?'

'Yes, really. It's not a job I would have picked but at least I didn't have to worry about where my next meal was coming from and I now have enough money to live well. After a while I bought into a business with an old Chinese woman.'

'Was that the food stall and café where we met?'

'Yup. I'm co-owner, not an assistant.'

'But you were still working in the…erm…in the brothel?'

'I had to. The contract my family signed was for five years and when I met Neil I had six months left. He bought me out of it.'

'Wow!' Mouse took a few seconds to consider this information. 'No, that can't be right. That's like some sort of modern day slavery! Nobody has the right to own someone. It's not right, definitely not right!'

Alice was pleasantly surprised that her new friend hadn't focussed on the subject of prostitution. 'So you're not bothered about me having been a prostitute then?'

'Not bothered about something that was forced upon you due to you and your family living in poverty? No, I'm not, Alice. It's not like it's your career of choice, is it?'

'And if it were?'

'Well that might be a problem, so I guess I may be a judgemental snob?'

Alice shook her head. 'You're most certainly neither of those. But to answer your question, Neil doesn't own me. He paid to get me out of my contract and we have an understanding that if we split up, I have no right to any of his money earned before our wedding and he has no right to any of mine.'

'So what do you get from the marriage if you were already financially independent and you would have been free to leave soon?'

'This might surprise you, Mouse, but Neil and I actually love each other.'

'I see.'

'I don't think you do.' She hesitated for a few moments. 'Nobody else in our community but Neil knows what I'm thinking about sharing with you. Can I trust you, Mouse?'

'If you have to ask, perhaps you can't,' Mouse replied. 'Rest assured that I won't repeat anything you've told me tonight, but please, don't tell me anything else if it makes you feel uncomfortable.'

Alice made a decision and talked. 'Neil started visiting every Friday and asked for me each time. We got to know each other, and after a few months, negotiations started. Neil was treated badly by his first wife and though, like most men, he enjoys sex, companionship is far more important to him. He's kind and thoughtful and treats me well. And after seeing the good and bad side of men, I'm glad to have someone who loves me for who I am, enjoys my company, and treats me like a lady. I love him, Mouse and I'm also grateful to him.'

'I understand and hope you'll be happy together for many years to come.'

'Thank you. Now what were you doing in the Walled City last week?'

It was such an unexpected change of subject that it totally threw Mouse. Alice had trusted her with her secret, so it was time for Mouse to return the favour. 'Trying to follow two soldiers who were up to no good,' she replied. 'But I got lost and a little bit scared and that's when your co-owner called me in to your café.'

'Ah, I see. But why would you want to play detective, Mouse?'

'I guess being curious is in my genes and I'm a bit bored to be honest. I need something to think about so I don't spend my spare time thinking about how unfair life can be.'

Alice could relate and felt she had an infinity with the woman sitting opposite. 'You do know the area's out of bounds to soldiers don't you? And that if you're caught in the Walled City you'll be investigated?'

'Yup. I also know it's out of bounds to dependants too, Alice.'

'Neil knows about my business and I'm not willing to give it up. It's slightly different for me.'

'How?' asked Mouse, trying to deflect attention onto Alice. Her new friend wasn't falling for it.

'Never mind that. How do you know these soldiers are up to no good?'

'The fact that one's a Gurkha and the other is a local and they're hanging out together is really unusual. I spoke to my brother about it and he said it just doesn't happen. Also, when I was here last night, they were in here with another soldier, I think he was a Gurkha officer. By the way he acted he was the boss. They went into that room there,' Mouse nodded towards the private room. 'Then they were joined by some Chinese mafia looking types and there was a kerfuffle and one of the mafia types came flying out of the door and his own boss, a big local bloke, knocked seven shades of…'

'Okay, okay, I get the picture. So you think because of that and the fact you've seen them in the Walled City means they're up to no good?'

'Yes, of course. It couldn't be more obvious to me.'

'I think you're right too, Mouse. But why haven't you just reported it?'

'Because it's hearsay, Alice. Their word against mine and if I bring it to the attention of anyone in authority, they could go underground and never be caught.'

'What about your new policeman friend, couldn't you tell him?'

'Err, no. It's our first date tomorrow and there's no way I'm going to speak to him about some suspicions I have. Not until I've found out more at the very least.'

The food arrived and they stopped talking for a while as Mouse watched the chicken tikka sizzle with the onions on the slate plate. The smell made her stomach rumble and she now realised how hungry she was.

'After you, Mouse.'

Alice smiled and they ate their starter in silence, savouring the creamy chicken and soft onions. Combined with the warmth of the many spices it was a memorable start to their dinner and apart from meeting Tony, Mouse was having the best time since her brother and his family had left.

Alice made a decision as the waiter took away the empty plates.

'It's not wise for you to wander around the Walled City on your own. Nothing good can come of it.'

'I'll be fine, Alice, honestly. If you knew what I've already been through in my life, you'd know I can look after myself.'

Alice resisted the urge to tell Mouse she was stupid and naïve. She didn't want anything to happen to this woman so had come up with a plan. 'If you ever need to follow these men or enter the Walled City for other reasons, call me and I'll come with you.'

'There's no need for…'

'There is every need, Mouse. That place is a den of murderers and thieves who wouldn't think twice about killing an English girl…'

'I'm Welsh…'

'Damn you! Killing anyone, Mouse. Foreigner, local, soldier, civilian – they don't discriminate! They want to protect their businesses and the influence of the triads extends to family members. You can bet your bottom dollar that if the Chinese soldier is working for them, they have some sort of pull over his family and will stop at nothing to ensure he does as he's told.'

Alice finished her rant and Mouse sat back to consider what she'd been told. Deep down she knew it was foolish of her, but she also knew that wouldn't stop her from trying to find out what was going on. But she didn't know her way around Hong Kong, and the Walled City was like a maze.

'Okay, I might need your help. But I don't want to get you into any danger or trouble.'

'You won't. Just promise me that you won't enter the Walled City without me.'

'But what if it's late at night, or you're working?'

'It doesn't matter, Mouse. Promise?'

'Yes, I promise.' Mouse wasn't even crossing her fingers and hoped this was a promise that she wouldn't break. Out of all the friends she'd expected to have in Hong Kong, a Thai ex prostitute hadn't been on her list.

They chatted about life in general as they finished their main course and agreed to meet the following week unless Mouse had reason to ask for Alice's help beforehand.

*****

Mouse had mixed emotions as Friday neared. Firstly, butterflies which turned to nervousness, then to anticipation followed by anxiety. On Thursday afternoon she started to feel guilty. She decided to get a sandwich from the Mess kitchen for lunch and was in the lift alone, talking to Guy, as she returned to her office on the 11th floor. 'I hope you don't mind, Guy. It's been a while and I'm …' She stopped talking as the lift door opened and the ADC stood aside to let her out.

'Who were you talking to Sergeant Halfpenny,' he asked.

'You caught me thinking out loud, Sir,' she said, slightly embarrassed but glad it was only the ADC and not anyone more important.

'You know you're as mad as a box of frogs?'

'Yes, Sir. Whatever you say, Sir.'

He laughed at her sarcasm and went off about his business.

I wish Guy would give me a sign that it's okay to date, she thought, as she entered her office and went about her business. Twenty minutes later, an unhappy looking brigadier stormed into his office with a worried looking Major Dickson, the SO2 Int, on his heels. He slammed the door and she didn't have to be discreet to listen. It was the first time she had heard Brigadier Harding-Brown raise his voice since she'd started working for him. From what she could glean from the one-sided conversation, he was talking about some sort of smuggling. As he got control of himself the volume decreased, and the conversation wasn't so easy to decipher. There was nobody else in the outer-office so Mouse closed the door. She convinced herself she was being a good PA and stopping any potential visitors from hearing the brigadier's business but it also enabled her to listen at the door without being caught. It was quiet for a few seconds and then she heard movement.

'And Bertie, if you breathe another word of this I'll come for you and I'll find a deserted high-rise building, open the fucking window and throw you straight out of it, even if I have to travel to wherever in the world you're going to be sent. Do you understand?' The brigadier was shouting again and Mouse rushed to be seated at her desk before the door opened.

'Yes, Sir,' A dejected Major Dickson replied. As he walked out of the office, Mouse busied herself at her workstation.

She closed the outer office doors behind him and went into the brigadier's office. 'Can I get you anything, Sir?'

'Only an SO2 Int who isn't a fuckwit!' he replied, and Mouse laughed.

The brigadier laughed with her, his bad temper seemingly disappearing. She was about to be really necky and ask questions, but saw that the boss was in deep thought, so kept quiet.

'There's smuggling going on,' he said, almost to himself, 'and we need to get to the bottom of it.'

'I see.' She didn't, but didn't want the boss to think she was totally thick.

'I don't think you do,' the brigadier replied. 'We have to find out how it's happening, Mouse, catch the perpetrators and stop it. All without bringing the British Forces into disrepute.'

'Has Major Dickson messed it up, Sir?'

'Major Dickson was only discussing it with his chums in the Officers Mess! They'll soon know we're onto them, whoever *they* are,' the brigadier said, and she could see he was winding himself up again. 'He's very lucky he's not getting court martialled, Mouse.'

'Yes, Sir.'

'I need to get rid of him. Get me the Deputy Military Secretary on the phone as soon as you can. It's going to be a late one for us tonight I'm afraid.'

'Yes, Sir. No problem.'

She rushed back to her desk and found the number she needed. Records Offices opened in the UK at eight thirty hours at the earliest, although some of the staff started work early. However, there was no guarantee that DMS would. Hong Kong was eight hours ahead of the UK, so she started phoning from sixteen hundred hours, on the off-chance that somebody might answer her call. She struck lucky.

'Brigadier Smith,' the clipped tones answered. He sounded like he was in the middle of something, so Mouse cut to the chase.

'Good morning, Sir. It's Sergeant Halfpenny from DCBF's office in Hong Kong. Brigadier Harding-Brown has asked to speak to you as a matter of urgency.'

'Put him on, Sergeant Halfpenny,'

She did as ordered and carried on with her work, knowing there was no way she could listen in to the call.

Ten minutes later the brigadier came out of his office, smirking and rubbing his hands together.

'Get Chief J2 and Major Dickson to come and see me, Mouse.'

She did as bid and Major Dickson appeared shortly after looking very sheepish, accompanied by the colonel who ran his branch. This was an interview without coffee, and she discovered later on that Major Dickson was being sent back to the home of the Intelligence Corps in Chicksands, to a future yet to be determined. *If Intelligence Corps personnel can't keep a secret, what hope do we have?* Mouse wondered when Major Dickson left the office. It was the last she would ever see of him.

The drama had given her something else to think about other than her date with Tony the following day and the distraction had cleared her head. Mouse now felt she could put things into perspective, and it was like a cloud had lifted. She would always love Guy but could make the choice of living in the past forever, or to get on with her life as she hoped he would want her to. As she left the office that evening, she decided on the latter and tried to let anticipation be the overriding emotion to occupy her mind for the next twenty-four hours.

Chapter 7 – More than a Feeling

After changing for the fourth time, Mouse decided on black trousers, boots – it was still monsoon season after all - and a red sparkly top that showed a little cleavage but not enough to make her look tarty. She looked in the mirror for one last time before leaving her room and smiled. 'Knock em dead, kiddo,' she told her reflection then closed the door and headed for the lift.

The walk over the bridge towards Hutchison House was the usual chaotic dodge fest, only this time it was worse as it seemed that everyone on Hong Kong island was heading in the opposite direction on this Friday evening. Feeling like a salmon swimming upstream, and after being bumped into for the third time, Mouse ducked into a shop and found their toilets. She didn't need to use the facilities, but did need her own space for a few minutes, knowing she'd be rude to the next person who bumped into her and didn't bother to apologise.

She carried on her journey when she calmed down and was the picture of serenity upon entering *The Bull and Bear*. The pub appeared full of Expat business types accompanied by few locals, who looked like they'd just finished work and decided on a few drinks before going home, or onto somewhere else. *Exactly like London*, thought Mouse. There were a few obvious tourists too, Brits by the look of them, dressed in shorts and t-shirts recently purchased from one of the local markets and visiting the British run pub because they wanted familiarity, or Friday night fish and chips.

Tony was at the bar placing an order and Mouse felt a twinge of jealousy when she witnessed the European-looking barmaid flirting with him. She gave herself a mental talking-to and plastered a smile on her face.

'Hi,' she said, as he looked up and saw her approaching.

'Hello, Mouse,' he said. 'Is this okay for you?' He lifted up a bottle of bubbly.

'Perfect, thanks,'

He inclined his head towards a table. 'Shall we?' Mouse followed Tony and the barmaid went about her business elsewhere.

'So is there anywhere in particular you'd like to go tonight?' he asked. 'I have a few suggestions if there isn't.'

'Fire away.'

'There's a curry house called Johnny's, not that far away.'

'The Officer's Mess Annex!' Mouse laughed. 'Or that's what I'm told it's known as.'

Tony smiled. 'You know that already?'

'Yeah. I haven't been there yet but I'm told it's pretty popular with our officers and their families.'

'And Chung King Mansions is popular with your guys too. Fab food there by the way.'

'Well that's somewhere I have been. Twice in fact. I met Alice there, last night. You know, Neil Mitchum's wife.' Mouse noticed the expression on Tony's face turn serious when she mentioned Alice. She thought it strange and waited for him to speak, but he didn't volunteer anything. 'We've arranged to meet up weekly,' she continued.

'That'll be fun for you both,' he said. 'She seems very nice.'

'Yeah, she's lovely. Do you know her, Tony?'

'I had met her before Sunday, yes.' He changed the subject. 'So, tonight then. If you don't fancy a curry, how do you fancy a show in the Hilton Hotel? They're usually quite intimate affairs and a lot of people are excited about this one as Tim Brooke-Taylor is acting in *An Inspector Calls.*'

Mouse let the stuff about Alice go, and gave him a questioning look.

'You know, one of the fellows from *The Goodies.*'

'Oh, that sounds fab. Will we be able to get tickets?'

'It was a bit presumptuous of me but-' He took an envelope out of his pocket and waved it in the air.

'Fabulous! But what if I'd fancied a curry?'

'I would have excused myself and phoned my friend at the hotel so someone else could have our seats. We don't have to be there for an hour so let's enjoy the champagne for now.' They clinked glasses. 'Dinner's included by the way.'

He must have been a mind reader as that was exactly what she was wondering. 'Great, I'm starving.'

Not much later, they made their way to the Hilton Hotel. Mouse was getting used to visiting four and five star hotels and didn't think she'd ever tire of sumptuous surroundings. There wasn't a proper stage. Instead, the stage area was in the middle of a semi-circle and the guests were seated at tables surrounding it, so they would almost feel part of the performance, as opposed to just viewing it. The first course was served – a choice between scallop shell pies, served in their shells and topped with flaky pastry, green silk handkerchiefs which were pasta made from spinach and tossed in a nutty brown butter and sage sauce, or mozzarella sticks with a spicy dipping sauce. They both opted for the mozzarella sticks.

'And a bottle of the house champagne,' added Tony.

They chatted while they waited for the food, the maitre'd having informed them that the performance would start after they'd finished their puddings and cheese and biscuits were served.

The starter was delicious, and Mouse struggled to decide whether to have steak au Poivre or the ballotine of turkey with potato rosti. A seafood lover, Tony opted for the grilled lobster, so Mouse finally decided on the turkey. By the time the dessert trolley arrived, she was stuffed to the gunnels and her date was surprised when she took a small piece of strawberry cheesecake.

'I don't want to offend anyone by not having anything.'

Tony chuckled at her comment and she gave his arm a playful punch. Their eyes made contact and she found it hard to look away. Her pulse quickened as Tony put a hand over hers and a long-forgotten feeling hit the pit of her stomach. A memory of Guy flitted into her mind and spoiled the moment. It was too soon and she needed to break the spell.

'How's your chocolate mousse?'

'What? Oh the mousse. Delicious, yeah.'

'And your cheesecake?'

'All the food's lovely, Tony, thanks. It's great and I'm looking forward to the show too. She sighed, knowing she needed to explain. 'Look, it's been ages since I've dated and I'm sorry if…'

'There's nothing to be sorry about. I haven't dated anyone for a while either, but for entirely different reasons to you. I'm so sorry you lost your husband, Mouse. I can't imagine how awful that must have been and under such terrible circumstances.'

'It's sometimes like it happened to another person. KC killed Guy and Becks, our lovely dog. I knew he was a bastard, Tony, but had no idea what he was really capable of. I thought I couldn't go on living but I know Guy would want me to live my life the best that I can, and I think I'm ready to move on now.'

'I hope so, Mouse. But I'm not going to rush you into anything. We'll see each other at your pace, and if it doesn't work out I'll be gutted.' He smiled wryly. 'But I'll always respect your wishes.'

His words put Mouse at her ease. She already wanted to believe he was a good man, and he'd just confirmed her thoughts. She also realised there was more to him than met the eye as he was obviously capable of tracking and catching sleazy criminals, if that was what he actually did. She was looking forward to discovering more about him and also the bits of his job he was willing to share. It would be like peeling layers off an onion but without the eye-watering moments. Letting her imagination run riot, Mouse smiled to herself.

'Penny for them?'

'Oh, it's nothing. I'm just happier than I've been in a while, that's all.' She blushed, worrying that she'd said too much. It was easy to let her guard down with this man.

'Me too, Mouse. Look, the show's about to start.'

Music filled the air and they looked towards the stage, expecting to see the actors. But before they appeared, Mouse sensed a presence behind them. Tony had noticed something too because the relaxed expression on his face changed. She gave him another questioning look, then turned.

It was the big Chinese man she'd seen in Chung King Mansions on Monday night, flanked by two of his flunkies. She had the same feeling she'd experienced on Monday – she'd seen this man somewhere before and it wasn't in Hong Kong. If only the memory would come to her.

The man gave Tony a wave and winked cheekily at Mouse. She quickly turned to look at Tony and his face was like thunder. He remained seated and watched as the man and his associates were shown to a table.

'What was all that about?'

'I'll tell you later,' he said as applause erupted from the other diners. The curtains opened to show a dining room scene with a man sitting in a chair reading a newspaper, and a woman sitting opposite him knitting. A doorbell rang and the woman put down her knitting and went to the door.

'Good evening, Inspector,' she said, and the audience clapped again as they realised the inspector was none other than one of the Goodies funny men, Tim-Brooke Taylor.

Mouse enjoyed the play while doing a little acting herself. Hoping she appeared suitably mesmerized, she occasionally sneaked a quick look at the men she now thought of as Chinese gangsters. They appeared to be enjoying the play as much as Tony and clapped, laughed or cheered in the appropriate places. She relaxed and enjoyed the rest of it, except for the message to the audience at the end, which she felt a bit patronising.

'Enjoy?' Tony asked when the final encore had taken place and the actors had left the stage.

'I did, until they decided to tell us all how to treat others. I wondered whether the message was directed at the triads over there?'

Tony knew exactly who she was talking about and laughed. 'Who knows? But you seemed to be fascinated by them.'

So he had noticed. 'Well it's not every day you get to see Chinese gangsters, Tony. And for me, it's twice in one week.' She explained about the fight on Monday night.

'But I thought you said you went for a curry with Alice on Tuesday night?'

'I did. But I have a rubbish sense of direction and wanted to recce the place first to make sure I could get there and back.'

'Seriously?'

'Yeah. I know and I'm embarrassed about it. But it's just the way I'm wired I guess. There's nothing wrong with my map reading by the way. It's my internal compass that doesn't work.

'I suppose that's one way of putting it. So how do you manage?'

'I use maps, do recces and bluff if I have to. But it doesn't affect the way I do my job. Anyway, the Chinese gangsters. When I saw the boss man on Monday night I had a feeling I'd seen him before.'

'I think you might be mistaken, Mouse. Not about him being a triad, you're right about that; his father's the boss of the 14K Triads. He's handed most of the reins over to his son who lords it around like he owns the place. They control a big part of the Walled City, and woe betide anyone who gets in their way. He's slippery as an eel and we haven't been able to pin anything on him, he inclined his head and raised an eyebrow, then continued, 'yet. But if I have my way, it's only a matter of time.'

'I thought it unlikely too, Tony. But there's something niggling in the back of my mind and I'm convinced I'm right. Hopefully it'll come to me sooner rather than later.'

She could tell that Tony was conflicted and struggling to believe her, but there was also something else. She could see it in his eyes.

'What is it?'

'I can't say too much, but I'm the 2IC of a team and our investigations are progressing quite well. That makes me dangerous to him.'

'That's great, Tony. Being able to get someone like that in prison where he belongs would be a coup for you and your team.'

'You're right, but like I just said, it would make me dangerous to him and his team.' He looked around. Everybody was engrossed in their own conversations but Tony wasn't comfortable discussing triads in such an insecure environment. He didn't want to make things awkward for Mouse by going back to the Mess, knowing how much her colleagues would gossip or whisper if they saw him. 'We can't talk about this here, Mouse. I've already been too indiscreet.'

'Walls have ears and all that,' she replied.

'Any suggestions?'

'There's no way we can go back to my room.'

'Would you come back to my flat? I know it's a bit presumptuous, but we'll be able to talk properly there without any interruptions.'

'I don't know, Tony, I-'

'I need to speak to you, and I promise I'll behave.'

They both laughed. She had no doubt he'd keep his promise, but Mouse was worried about whether she would be able to behave, never mind Tony.

'Okay.'

He signalled a waiter for the bill, then thanked the staff and paid, refusing to take anything from Mouse. 'We can go Dutch next time if you insist,' he said, both knowing there would definitely be a next time.

The gangster made a point of raising his hand in a wave as they left the hotel. Mouse believed he was sticking his fingers up at Tony, but Tony knew it was his way of saying he'd clocked his new companion and it was a warning.

They made their way to the police flats in the Mid-Levels.

'I first lived above the police station in our accommodation. This was very much like your Sergeants Mess set up where we had a communal dining-room, ante-room and bar area and we were fed from a communal kitchen. Each of us had a small flat with a bedroom, living room and bathroom. I moved on promotion and now have a self-contained flat but in a gated community. There are lots of us living in this complex and we have an amah who cleans for us, and cooks for us too, if required. Like I said, our community is gated and is discreetly guarded by armed members of the Hong Kong Police.'

'Here we are.' Tony keyed in the number on the locked gate and they walked in and buzzed the building. As they entered, Mouse thought it was just like going into HMS Tamar and knew the police would be as used to the entry process as she and her military colleagues were.

They went up to the tenth floor and entered Tony's flat.

'Fancy champagne, or something else?'

'Champers would be lovely, thanks. Do you always have that in your fridge, just in case?'

'Now that would be telling.' He grinned. 'Make yourself comfortable while I get the drinks. It's not a bad view.' He nodded towards the window and Mouse wandered over.

The near view was of the numerous restaurants, street eateries and the shopping malls that were accessed by the outdoor, partly covered escalators than ran from the end of the Central District all the way up to the Mid-Levels. People were going about their business and it wasn't the first time that Mouse made the comparison with people and ants, both concentrating so much on their own business that they didn't stop to take a look at the world around or above them. Though from the tenth floor, the people did look bigger than ants. She stopped letting her thoughts wander and looked out into the distance towards the many other high-rise buildings that drew the eye by their neon lights. The harbour was beyond these buildings but couldn't be seen when it was dark. Mouse wondered how long it would be until she spent a night with Tony, and he showed her the view in daylight. She thought about Guy for a second and felt a guilty pang. It would happen, but not tonight. Definitely not tonight.

'Here you go.' He returned with two glasses and the champagne under one arm. Mouse took a glass, then Tony put the bottle on a coaster on the coffee table. 'Cheers, Mouse.'

'Cheers.' They chinked glasses and both took a sip. 'The food, the show and the company tonight has been wonderful,' she said. 'Especially the company.'

'Most definitely,' he replied. 'It's just a shame the local criminal fraternity decided to spoil it.'

'They haven't spoiled it for me, Tony.'

'That's only because you don't know the full story. I'm not sure we should be drinking champagne when you hear what I have to tell you. Come and sit down, Mouse.'

With the weight of the world on his shoulders, he plonked himself onto one of the hardback chairs and Mouse perched on the settee opposite.

'I mentioned earlier that I hadn't dated anyone in ages. What I haven't told you was that the last girl I went out with returned to England to work.'

'Oh. I'm sorry to hear that. Were you…'

'We didn't split up because she wanted to work in England, Mouse. She returned to England because she received a threat.'

'A threat? What, from one of the triads you were trying to catch?'

'Exactly.' He inclined his head and raised his eyebrows, impressed she'd worked it out so quickly. 'Penny, that was her name by the way, was in a bar with her friends one night when three men, dressed in black suits and white shirts - their usual gear - walked in, ordered shots, and downed them. She told me they looked around, came over to her table and one of them put his hand in his pocket, like he was going to take something out. He came out empty-handed but pointed two of his fingers at her, like a gun. Then he grinned, said, 'Bang!', blew on his fingers and put his hand back in his pocket. She was terrified, especially when one of the others leaned over the table and said into her face, 'You're dead!'. Then they all laughed and walked out.'

'And that made her leave Hong Kong?'

'Yup. I explained they were just trying to frighten her, and they wouldn't do anything to her, unless she ventured into the Walled City-and that was never going to happen-but it spooked her so much that she decided to leave. That was after accusing me of being a maverick and playing with other people's lives.'

'Oh, Tony, that's awful. I'm so sorry.'

'I couldn't believe that one single incident would make her believe that they'd kill her. Seriously, Mouse that wouldn't happen outside of the Walled City. These people have a wide network of criminal contacts but generally keep to their own areas. They do, however, turn the screws on family members of those who refuse to fall into line. Emotional blackmail usually does the trick in my experience.'

'How?'

'The easy way to threaten someone who doesn't pay their monthly fees or whatever else the triads want from them is to threaten the ones they love. It works well and is a well-known way of doing business. London gangsters do this, the Italian mafia, triads and also the IRA, amongst others. That's one of the reasons I'm here, and others like me. Although some of them operate worldwide, it would be more difficult for them to reach my family in the UK without being caught so they don't have much leverage to blackmail or coerce me.'

'But now those men have seen me out with you, you're worried they might try to threaten me so they can get to you?'

'I would be, Mouse, if I knew the Walled City wasn't out of bounds to you. Promise me you won't go in there...'

'Oh God!' Mouse had a sudden memory and a picture appeared in her mind, as clear as day.

'I'm sorry, Mouse. I know it's awful and will understand if you don't want to see me anymore.'

'What?'

'Your reaction. It's understandable and after what happened to your husband, I totally...'

'It's nothing to do with that, Tony. I just remembered where I saw the triad man. Have you heard of Melham, in London?'

'Oh yes. There's a cartel of criminals there well known to us. Another lot as slippery as fish. The Cartwrights.'

'I know. Do you know Earl?'

'Oh yes. He's another Mr Teflon, as much as the Special Branch in the Met tried to catch him. He always had an alibi. How do you…?'

'I know him. Quite well actually. And he helped me when I needed it most.'

'So the woman I hoped to be with is an associate of a well-known London gangster. Oh fuck!' Tony put his head in his hands. 'I can't believe this, Mouse. I just can't fucking believe it!'

She hadn't expected a good reaction, but this totally shocked her. 'Earl was a small part of my past, Tony. I knew him by chance, that's all. It's not like I went out of my way to get to know a gangster!'

He lifted his head and shook it slowly. She waited for him to say *I'm disappointed in you,* or some such cliché as the warm feeling from earlier that evening had completely disappeared, leaving a knot of disappointment and sadness in its place.

'I think I'd better go.'

'I'll see you back to the Mess. Mouse, I need some time to process…'

The sound of the door banging closed behind her drowned out any further words.

The streets were still packed – it didn't matter the time of day, Hong Kong was always busy. Mouse concentrated on getting herself back to the Mess in one piece. She was on auto pilot and instead of people watching like she usually did, her head was down, and she went about her own business without a care for anyone else. She didn't realise she was being followed and it was debatable whether she would have realised, had she been alert. He stopped following her when she arrived at HMS Tamar, ducked into a shop and made a short call before he disappeared back into the crowds.

Mouse cried herself to sleep.

For the first time since his death, these tears had nothing to do with her late husband.

Chapter 8 – Alone Again

Her phone was ringing as she got ready to leave her room just after ten o'clock the following morning. Mouse ignored it, even though whoever was calling tried several more times, and she went out a few minutes later with the phone still ringing. She reflected on the few frogs she had met and now, the one who seemed to have been a prince had turned out to be a flaming toad. She sighed. What would have been her first serious relationship since Guy, had ended almost before it began, and she was bitterly disappointed.

I'll meet Alice once a week and that's enough, she resolved, and decided to spend the weekend sightseeing and taking in everything Hong Kong had to offer. She started with the island side, deciding to visit the Peak.

Luck was on her side and it was a clear day. She got on the funicular Peak Tram and sat on the right to get the best views, as she'd heard people say. As she travelled the steep gradient, she marvelled at the sights all around her. The higher she went, the more of the island she could see, and Mouse oooh'd and aaah'd to herself, at each of the amazing sights. She could see the whole Hong Kong skyline as the tram slowly made its way up, stopping to pick up more passengers on the way. The high-rise buildings surrounding the harbour became smaller the higher the tram went but she could still make out the distinctive outline of the HSBC Bank Building. What she found even more amazing were some of the houses, the gardens and fences that could be seen from the train. Space was at a premium in Hong Kong and most families were squashed into two, or even one small room, and paid high rents for the privilege. She'd been told that all of the rich folk lived up the Peak but seeing was believing. The homes she could see looked like the millionaire mansions she'd seen on TV shows about celebrities and their families, and she could only imagine the extreme wealth of the people who lived in these places.

'Amazing, place, honey, isn't it?' said a big man sitting opposite her. 'The views, I mean. So much packed into such a small place.' It was obvious he was a tourist from his summer clothes and American accent.

'Are you visiting Hong Kong?' The woman sitting next to him asked, and Mouse replied that she was, rather than telling them her real reason for being on the island. They tried to engage her in friendly banter, but she simply wasn't in the mood. Usually polite, she gave short answers to their questions and saw the woman roll her eyes at her husband when she thought Mouse wasn't looking. Eventually they gave up, and Mouse looked around the carriage at the other passengers. All except one were dressed like tourists. There were even some people who looked like locals. But a local man who was dressed in long trousers and a plain blue shirt stood out like a sore thumb. He was wearing sunglasses and, like the others, was looking out at the views. He had a pager on his belt and carried a bag. She wondered if he worked in, or had anything to do with one of the businesses on the Peak, but her gut instinct sent alarm bells ringing. *Something's not right,* she thought, deciding to give him a wide berth.

They arrived at the top shortly after and were shepherded off the tram directly into the shopping area.

'Man trouble I expect.' She heard the American say to her husband, obviously thinking she was speaking quietly, but a number of people looked around at her and the woman coughed to hide her embarrassment. Still grumpy, Mouse frowned but carried on walking without turning around.

Like locals everywhere, she knew hawkers and business owners would take every opportunity to make money out of tourists, so assumed the prices in the Peak shops would be inflated. Looking around, Mouse was soon proved right. She smiled politely at the calls of, 'Copy watch, Missy,' or 'Pretty jewellery, just for you, Missy,' and also calls of 'Wha you want? We make you anything.' She plastered a false smile on her face and walked past them all, saying an occasional, 'No thank you,' as she made her way out into the circular viewing area. She spent time walking around slowly and feeding the telescopic viewing machines with dollar after dollar when the money ran out, to give her close up as well as distant views. It didn't take long before her senses went into overload and she'd had her fill. She was then drawn to a book in the viewing area that was under cover in case of inclement weather. When she opened it, she found the writing was in English and noticed it was a book for duty policemen to sign, showing what time they'd visited during their shift. She let out a chuckle when reading a comment that said: *Lovely views thank you,* from a woman who signed herself as *Norma from Glasgow.* Laughing lifted her mood, and Mouse suddenly felt grateful for her experience and that during her unplanned journey it had been a clear day. These views would stay with her for some time, and she mentally ticked the Peak off her 'things to do' list.

Now feeling calmer and slightly more sociable, she made her way back to the tram for the journey down, buying a tacky t-towel with pictures of the Peak, from a shopkeeper on her way.

Her guard went up again when she noticed the man dressed in trousers and blue shirt was in the carriage on the way down but didn't see any of the others who had been passengers on the way up. As they alighted at the bottom, he seemed to hold back. Thinking she was becoming paranoid after what Tony had told her the night before, Mouse decided to carry on about her business and headed for Poor Man's Market. Dodging the crowds had become second nature and walking helped to clear her head, so she proceeded on foot.

She didn't particularly need anything, but that had never stopped her from shopping in the past. With everything else that had been going on, Mouse had forgotten that an American Navy ship had docked in Hong Kong the day before and the sailors would now be on shore leave. Shortly after she heard a few American accents and the streets were peppered with some fit-looking men with short haircuts and loud voices. They were dressed in civvies but stood out like sore thumbs. During the induction briefings, British military personnel were informed not to shop when the American ships were in as local businesses inflated their prices. The value of Hong Kong dollars had the same value as American dollars during these periods and the locals charged the same to all foreigners, not just the Americans. For their part, the American sailors seemed quite happy to pay these prices, but the Brits certainly were not.

Mouse walked around the market, refusing to pay the outrageous prices when asked. She saw a crowd of people clustered around one vendor and she wondered what was going on. Taking a peek, she wished she hadn't bothered. A Cantonese vendor had a bucket full of live frogs in front of his legs. As she watched, he plucked one from from the bucket and unceremoniously chopped off its legs, then dropped them into a frying pan full of hot fat. It sizzled. She held back nausea as she watched the vendor throw the body of the frog into another bucket, where it rested along with the remains of the other poor creatures already in there.

'Yuck,' she said out loud, and now, having lost her appetite for any sort of shopping, Mouse made her way out of the market and wandered around. Her aim was to become totally immersed in the sights, sounds and smells of Hong Kong to try and blot out her disappointment over what might have been. The visit to the Peak had done the trick, but now the memories of last night's meal with Tony were flickering in and out of her mind.

'Damn you!' Mouse said aloud, stopping suddenly.

'Ay ya!' said a voice behind her as a woman walked directly into her back. Mouse turned in irritation to have a go, but the woman had already moved on. Out of her peripheral vision she saw a man duck into a shop doorway. It was only a fleeting glimpse, but she recognised the blue shirt and knew it was the same man she had seen on the tram. *Why would Tony arrange to have me followed if we're not together?* she wondered, as she hurried into the shop to confront the man.

However, she couldn't see him and left a few minutes later deciding to treat herself to afternoon tea at the Marriott Hotel in Pacific Place. The hotel was American owned but she'd heard their teas could rival any British establishment.

Mouse asked for one of the smaller semi-circular booths towards the rear of the restaurant. She could have the best of both worlds there, seeing people coming and going and also having a bit of privacy. When she wasn't people watching, she read her book and sipped her lemon tea while she waited for the food to arrive. Soon, a waiter delivered beautiful silver salvers with small sandwiches of salmon and cucumber, York ham with tomato dressing and a selection of small cheeses accompanied by miniature crackers and seedless grapes. The top tier of the salver had a number of delicate dessert cakes. She'd ordered afternoon tea for one but there was enough there to make three people very happy.

As much as she enjoyed the food and surroundings Mouse couldn't stop her mind from wondering, both about Tony, and about the man who had been following her. *That's it!* she whispered when it came to her; he'd arranged to have her followed because the triad people had seen them together and didn't know they weren't a couple. So Tony was thinking of her safety, even though he didn't want to see her anymore. *He's got a flaming cheek*, she thought. As much as she wanted to tell him so, her stubbornness wouldn't allow it, so she decided to put up with it for now, and find a third party to contact him for her. Aware that Tony and Alice knew each other better than they acted when they were in each other's company, Mouse didn't want either to know that she knew, so she didn't feel she could ask Alice to give him a message from her. She assumed Alice was an informant for Tony and she would just have to find another way to get a message to him. In the meantime, she would try to give her new stalker a run for his money.

She didn't see him when she left the Marriott and wondered if somebody else had replaced him. Mouse looked for likely candidates but eventually convinced herself that nobody was following her. What she didn't know was that her new follower was more able than the man in the blue shirt, and had absolutely nothing to do with Tony, or his colleagues in the Hong Kong Police.

*****

As much as Mouse submerged herself in her work during the next few months, she couldn't get Tony out of her mind. It was most irritating, but it didn't stop her from taking her phone off the hook most nights, so she didn't have to listen to it ringing incessantly when she was in her room. She enjoyed her weekly meets with Alice, and they decided that if Mouse needed to speak to her at short notice while she was at work, she would call the Seven Eleven shop two doors down from where Alice worked. Most of the shops in Hong Kong had phones that customers could use, and all local calls were free. 'My friend works there, and I've already told her to come find me if you phone. Just ask for Malee, they will all understand that.'

Mouse hadn't had cause to visit the Walled City since she'd got lost in there, but a series of events would put her back on the trail of the Chinese and Gurkha soldiers and lead her to the forbidden area.

She carried on exploring during the weekends and even her fascination with Hong Kong couldn't dampen the loneliness she was starting to feel. Part of the following weekend was already taken as the current Garrison Sergeant Major had been selected for a commission and was due to return to the UK. His dining out from the Sergeants Mess would take place on Friday evening. Mouse hadn't been to a Regimental Dinner in a while and was looking forward to it. She had the work week to get through first and on the Monday morning, everything turned to ratshit. She was awoken by her ringing phone at five thirty hours. She had remnants of a dream about Tony in her head as she sleepily picked up the phone.

'Hello,'

'Is that Sergeant Halfpenny?'

'Yes, it is.'

'This is the duty officer. DCBF has told me to contact you. He wants the office opened and everything good to go by zero six hundred hours. I know CBF's PA is on leave, but is she local?'

He should look at his contact list, Mouse thought, now fully awake, but she kept her mouth shut. 'She's gone to the UK, Sir and won't be back until next week.'

'Damn!'

'I could phone Q Mitchum instead, Sir. If it's all hands to the deck, he will help out.'

'Good idea, Sergeant Halfpenny, I'll do that while you get yourself to the office ASP.'

'Will do, Sir, but what's happened?'

'One of our officers has been murdered and the press are going to be all over it like a tramp on chips, so jump to it.'

Jump to it, indeed! 'Yes, Sir. Will do.'

She had a quick shower and dressed, and Mouse was opening the corridor door and suite of offices ten minutes ahead of time. The cleaner didn't put the coffee machine on until seven thirty, so as soon as everything was open and the machines fired up, she filled the percolator and the smell of strong coffee wafted through the waiting area not much later. It was generally too strong for her, but Mouse thought she might need it today, so she helped herself to the first coffee from the pot and was sitting at her desk when the general and ADC arrived at twenty minutes past the hour.

'Morning Sir,' she said, standing up. 'Coffee?'

'The ADC will get it thanks. Come into my office with your notepad. The MA will be here within the next thirty minutes and I want you to take some orders for him before then. Rupert,' he addressed the ADC, 'bring me a brew and as soon as the brigadier gets in, tell him to come into my office.'

'Yes, Sir,' the ADC replied as Mouse followed the general into his office.

'Shocking business,' said the general, shaking his head.

'Yes, Sir,' Mouse replied.

'Get the Provost Marshal and SO1 Media Ops here as soon as you can. You and Q Mitchum man the phones. Be polite to local press that call, but don't tell them anything at this stage, until we know what's happened.'

'Yes, Sir. Can I just ask the officer's…'

'Captain Gurung based at Gun Club Hill Barracks. His family are being consoled now. Terrible business.'

The door opened and her brigadier walked in with a, 'Morning General.'

'Miles,' the general nodded. 'Sit down, today's going to be a rollercoaster. This is what we know so far.'

Mouse heard the start of the general's conversation and was shocked that one of the Gurkha officers had had his throat slit by a kukri – the curved knife used in Asia and issued to all Gurkha soldiers. It seemed obvious that the perpetrator must have been a Gurkha soldier as they were all issued with the knives. She was rushed off her feet for most of the day taking calls from the civvy press during the first few hours of the morning. The SO1 Media Ops had set up an emergency media cell, so by nine o'clock, she was able to tell any callers to ring that extension. It was impossible to get on with any of her own routine work while the phones kept ringing off the hook. CBF and DCBF had decided to visit the crime scene, along with the Provost Marshal.

'We'll be working with the local police on this,' DCBF had told the Provost Marshal, 'and I want full cooperation. We have nothing to hide.'

'Yes, Sir. I'll brief the troops,' the colonel responded.

Make sure you and Q man the phones, Sergeant Halfpenny,' said the MA as the group were leaving the office, 'and call me at Gun Club Hill Barracks if there's anything urgent.'

'Yes, Sir,' she replied. After the chaotic morning so far, it was good to take a deep breath and have a few moments to herself. She knew this was just a brief respite and decided to clear the general's office while the phones weren't ringing. Mouse grabbed a tray and started stacking the crockery. Her eyes were drawn to a blue folder on CBF's desk which she knew was none of her business, but that had never stopped her before.

Quickly checking that nobody was outside, she closed the doors to the outer office and went back into the general's room. The folder contained the initial report of what had happened, and some gruesome photos of the dead man. Mouse was shocked. Not only because of the way the captain had been murdered, but also because she recognised him as the man she had assumed was in charge of the two soldiers she had seen that night in the Sheri-Punjab restaurant at Chung King Mansions. She took a step back and stared at the folder. Did the chain of command know about his association with the two junior ranks? Did they know about the triad connection? And was he murdered by one of his own, or a triad? She quickly scanned the report. Captain Gurung was under investigation for smuggling gold out of Hong Kong to Nepal and the UK.

'Oh, my God!' Mouse said, shocked. She read on. The chain of command believed that the gold was smuggled in the MFO boxes of soldiers who were posted from Hong Kong. Mouse knew duty officers were appointed to do random checks but it appeared that when he was on duty, Captain Gurung had not been checking properly. The report said that an unnamed British Officer was also suspected and that investigations were ongoing. She put the folder back exactly as she had found it and opened the office again as quickly as she could. This information was dynamite, and she wondered why it had just been left on CBF's desk for anyone to read. Correction. *The only personnel allowed in this office were his personal staff and they were trusted.* That thought made her feel better and she cleared the office and closed the door, deciding that she would guard his office like a Rotweiler and not allow anyone in there until CBF and his personal staff returned.

Q Mitchum returned from his smoke break shortly after and Mouse wondered how she was going to keep him out of the general's office.

'Can you manage in here now that things have calmed down, Mouse?'

'Yes, of course.'

'Good, 'cause they want me to organise the media cell manning and rosters and all that,' he said.

'No problem, Q, it's quietened down a bit now anyway. If I need any help can I borrow Corporal H?'

'Yes, I'll brief him. By the way, Alice said she can do Wednesday night instead of tonight if you're too knackered after you finish today.'

With all the events of the morning so far, Mouse had completely forgotten she was meant to be meeting Alice on Monday this week, instead of Tuesday, as Alice had some other plan for tomorrow night.

'Oh thanks. That would be much better. Can you tell her the usual place on Wednesday then instead, or shall I phone her?'

'No probs, Mouse. I'll let her know.' And with that, he left the office.

This day was full of shocks and surprises and another one arrived that afternoon. The general and the others returned to the office shortly before lunch time.

'Order lunches from the Mess, Sergeant Halfpenny, please.'

'Already done, Sir,' she replied to the MA, trying not to look too smug. 'I've asked for five.'

'Well, you'd better get another two, and something for yourself. We have two visitors from the Hong Kong Police arriving at thirteen hundred hours.'

'Yes, Sir.'

The Officers Mess staff said they'd deliver the trays, and shortly after she busied herself taking them into the general's office along with the crockery and refreshments for everyone. Just before thirteen hundred, Mouse took a call from the Security Station in the lobby informing her that one of the guards was escorting two officers from the Hong Kong Police up to the Command Group office suite. The lift pinged as she put down the phone and left her desk, making her way there. The guard stayed in the lift as the two men walked out and Mouse tried, but failed, to hide her surprise.

'This is Sergeant Halfpenny, Guv,' Tony said to his boss and Mouse held out her hand.

'DCI Carpenter,' the man said, giving her hand a vigorous shake. 'And you already know DS Dryden I believe?'

'Yes, Sir, we've met. Follow me, gentlemen please.'

136

They did as bid, and Mouse made the introductions before the MA asked the DCI to go into the general's office.

'Would you like tea or coffee?' she asked Tony with a sweet, polite smile.

'Coffee would be lovely, thanks. I'll give you a hand.'

'I can manage thanks.' Mouse headed for the corridor, but he followed her anyway.

'We need to talk,' Tony said quietly.

'You've made your position perfectly clear,' she said. 'I don't think there's anything else to discuss.'

'But I didn't make my position very clear. You left before I had a chance to do so and have refused to take any of my calls. It's all very childish, Mouse.'

'Childish! Childish? You made an assumption then tried telling me who I can and cannot speak to, on our first date for God's sake, and you have the audacity to call me childish! You controlling, manipulative...'

The sound of a polite cough interrupted her and they both turned to see the ADC standing there.

'Your boss needs you, DS Dryden.'

'Here's your coffee,' Mouse shoved the cup and saucer towards Tony who gave her a thunderous look before following the ADC into the general's office.

She was still smarting from being called childish less than an hour later when she heard movement within the general's office. She had no desire to play *Mrs Polite* when the visitors left.

'I need the ladies,' she said to the ADC. 'Can you escort them downstairs, Sir?' She knew it was unprofessional but didn't give a hoot.

'No problem,' he said, and Mouse disappeared from the office before the visitors came out of the general's office.

The next few days in the office were manic. When she wasn't concentrating on work, her mind alternated between thinking about Tony and wondering whether she should do anything with the information she had about the Chinese and Gurkha corporal. She knew the evidence was circumstantial so decided to carry out her own investigations. Despite coming to a decision to never see Tony again, Mouse did her best to hide her disappointment when the phone in her room stopped ringing. She had to find more to do in her down time to take her mind off that irritating man. She always had fun at the weekly dinner with Alice, but now recognised she needed something more in her life. Although she loved Hong Kong, she wasn't sure about the job and now she knew the office routines and what was required, found it all a bit mentally unchallenging and boring. It was awful that murder and its ensuing chaos had taken away that boredom, and that made her feel guilty. *What sort of person does that make me?* she asked herself, not really wanting to know the answer. As far as the job was concerned, she knew she would stick it for a while due to the risks she'd taken to get posted to Hong Kong in the first place. No husband, no dog, no new relationship, few friends and no strong desire to stay put, meant spare time. She was fed up of having too much time to think so she wanted to make plans to make her stay in Hong Kong more eventful.

*****

Mouse was getting ready to go out on Wednesday night when the phone in her room rang.

'It's me, I'm full of a cold and can't make it tonight, sorry,' said Alice. 'I've taken tomorrow and Friday off too.'

'Ooh, you poor thing. It must be bad for you to take time off.' Alice's work ethic was phenomenal so Mouse knew she must have been really ill to take time off.

'Do you need anything? Shall I come round and help?' she asked, recalling Alice telling her that Neil was pretty useless around the home, despite his best efforts.

'It's okay thanks, Mouse. I made some soup and we can always get takeaways. I just have to let this run its course. I'll call you during the weekend and have a great night on Friday.'

'I'll certainly try. But you look after yourself and concentrate on getting better. And you know where I am if you need me.'

They hung up and Mouse thought about the forthcoming dinner night on Friday. The Garrison Sergeant

Major was being commissioned into the Grenadier Guards and this was to be his last function. As much as she'd been looking forward to it, the events of the week had dampened her spirits and she was no longer in the mood for a Reggy Dinner this week but knew there was no way of getting out of it. Mouse sighed then gave herself a mental shake. Grabbing her coat, she decided to go out for a quick and cheap dinner, come back to her room to watch some crap TV, then have an early night. *I'm so rock and roll,* she thought and smiled to herself as she closed the door behind her.

First thing Thursday morning the Garrison Sergeant Major phoned. 'Morning, Sir,' she said when she recognised his voice, hoping he wanted to speak to the brigadier. He didn't.

'We have some guest speakers at my dinner on Friday, Sergeant Halfpenny, and I want you to host one of them.'

Bloody great! that's all I need. 'Yes, Sir,' she replied. 'Who is it?'

'They're going to speak to us about crime and corruption. Be in the lobby to meet them at eighteen fifty hours, tomorrow.'

'Will do, Sir. Who else is hosting and who are the guests?'

'They're due to arrive at nineteen hundred so I'll brief you beforehand.'

'Yes, Sir,' she replied, but the GSM had already gone.

So not only did she have to attend a dinner she didn't want to, but she had to host a guest who was going to bore all the mess members with stories of crime and corruption. Like they didn't know all about that in Hong Kong anyway. He'd probably be a crusty old fart who loved the sound of his own voice and she would be expected to laugh at his unfunny jokes.

'Morning, Mouse.' The brigadier walked into the office, full of the joys. 'Penny for them?'

'Nothing that would interest you, Sir. Coffee?'

He laughed, she went to get his brew, and the work day commenced.

*****

Mouse was in the lobby five minutes earlier than ordered, knowing what a stickler the GSM was for being on time. It was the first time she'd worn her tropical mess kit and her body was toned from the aerobics classes and the swimming.

WO1 Gary Sutherland was already there. He wolf-whistled. 'You scrub up well, Mouse.' He approached her and went to put an arm around her. Mouse backed away but it didn't stop him. 'Anytime you fancy getting to know me better, just give me a call. I'll drop everything.' He winked and she was repulsed.

'I'm sure Mrs Sutherland would be delighted to hear what a loving and faithful husband she has,' she said with a smile, omitting the courtesy of calling him Sir. He might be a warrant officer class one, but she certainly wasn't going to give him any respect if he thought it all right to come on to her.

A few other mess members arrived, and Mouse thought they looked a smart bunch in their Navy, Army and Air Force mess kits. They turned as one when they heard the lift and the GSM arrived.

'We have four guests. Mr Sutherland will sit on the left of the general and I'll be on his right. The ASM will sit next to the MA, and Flight Sergeant Masters keep an eye out from your end of the table to make sure their glasses are always full.'

Flight Sergeant Masters was in charge of the entertainments committee and he replied with a crisp. 'Yes, Sir,' before the GSM continued. 'Our other guests are two civvy coppers who CBF wanted the Sergeants Mess to receive a brief from. We both thought it a good idea for them to present to the mess before my dinner while everyone still has their faculties about them. I know DCI Carpenter of old and we go back a long way. His DS is a good bloke too. So, I'm going to host the DCI, and Sergeant Halfpenny, the DS.'

Shit, thought Mouse, trying to keep her expression neutral. Her mind was working overtime trying to find a way out of attending the dinner, but she knew it was impossible. It was usually the more senior mess members who hosted guests unless they specifically wanted a woman to host, so she assumed that was his reasoning and realised she would just have to grin and bear it. Tony was to be a guest of the mess so it wasn't like she could be rude to him or ignore him, and he would be well aware of that.

'Let's give them a night they'll never forget in the best club in the British military.'

'Yes, Sir.' The senior NCOs replied, and the warrant officers nodded in agreement.

CBF and his MA arrived at the same time as DCI Carpenter and Tony. They walked in chatting amicably until they heard the GSM's voice.

'Welcome, Sirs,' he said and did the introductions. 'Please follow me to the Sergeants Mess - the best mess in the British Army.'

'I don't know about that GSM,' said the MA.

'I'm not even in the Officers Mess yet, Sir, but know for a fact I'm right. And I intend to show you tonight just how right I am.'

The GSM went in the lift with the General, MA, DCI Carpenter and WO1 Sutherland. Mouse was left with Tony, the flight sergeant and a few of the Navy senior rates.

'I hope you're looking forward to this evening,' she asked him in clipped tones and with a forced smile.

'Very much so, Mouse.'

She heard a few sniggers from two of the seniors standing behind her and turned. 'Something funny?' she asked, and they laughed again without saying a word.

The lift opened and they entered the Sergeants Mess. A waitress in a black skirt and white blouse held a tray of drinks.

'Wine, beer, gin, vodka or a soft drink, Tony?' she asked in the same clipped tone.

Tony picked up an orange juice and thanked the waitress, deciding to ignore the tone Mouse used. She picked up a glass of wine.

'How are you?' he asked, as they sipped their drinks.

'I'm very well, thank you. It's been an extremely busy week at work as you're well aware, but it's good to be busy. Everything's fine. And how are you?' she asked sweetly.

'No, seriously, how are you?'

'Seriously, I am fine. How are you?' Mouse asked, wondering which one of them would lose patience first.

'I'm quite pissed off, Mouse, if you really want to know.'

'To be honest, Tony, I don't. Can you try to look as if you're enjoying yourself, just a little bit please? The GSM is looking at us and if he thinks I'm not hosting you properly I'll be in the shit.'

'I'll make a deal with you.' Now Tony gave a false smile. 'If you stop being so evasive and bloody difficult, I promise I'll try to look as if I'm having fun. How does that sound?'

The GSM approached so she didn't need to respond. 'I hope Sergeant Halfpenny's looking after you, Tony?'

'Oh, yes, Ollie, she's being her usual charming self.'

The GSM looked from Tony to Mouse, trying to work out what was going on.

'Aren't you, Mouse,' Tony added.

'As if, Tony. The DS is regaling me with tales of his more interesting busts, Sir. Fascinating stuff and I can't wait to hear the presentations.'

'Glad to hear it, Sergeant Halfpenny. You can tell me all about it in my office Monday morning.'

'But, Sir, the brigadier…'

'I'm sure the brigadier can spare you for fifteen minutes.'

'Yes, Sir,'

The sound of the gong got their attention. 'Ladies and gentlemen, five minutes to dinner,' announced the Mess Manager and drinks were put aside as guests and Mess Members rushed to the toilets. As was mess tradition, if guests or mess members left the table during dinner to use the bathrooms, they would be fined a bottle of port and named and shamed on their return. This could result in months of ribbing from their colleagues, so most did their best to avoid the situation.

Being a sergeant, Mouse was seated towards the bottom of the tables and was surprised that Tony was put next to her, albeit on her right, nearer the top table. She listened to the presentation from his DCI, with him chirping in when asked. He was also in charge of the visual display which was shown on the large projector screen. Some of the slides were quite vicious, showing pictures of locals who had been murdered, tortured or beaten up.

'If there was ever any doubt about whether family members are safe, I think these images speak for themselves. The triads, like most other organised criminals, threaten families of their victims in order to get their own way. They have government officials and police in their pockets ,too. Make no bones about it, ladies and gentlemen, we're at war with these people, some battles we win but others...' He left the words hanging.

'Any information you have that may help us fight this battle, no matter how trivial it may seem, should be brought to our attention at the earliest opportunity. Encourage your subordinates and superiors to do this, too, and, excuse me general, but it doesn't have to go through your chain of command if you're more comfortable coming directly to us.'

Mouse looked at the general who had leaned in to whisper something to the GSM. They clearly had their views about what should and should not go through the chain of command and she could guess what they were. The DCI continued talking and the top table decided not to interrupt his presentation. She guessed a directive would be issued about this in due course.

'Thank you for listening, ladies and gentlemen, that concludes my presentation and I'll now answer any questions.'

'How many gangs are in Hong Kong and is it true they'll all in the Walled City?' asked one of the Chief Petty Officers.

'Yes, the majority of these people live there, and we know the K14 and a number of others operate within those confines. But they also operate outside and we're constantly trying to stop their drug and people trafficking.'

Instead of being bored, Mouse found it fascinating, and the DCI's words about passing on information resonated with her. She knew she had to find out more about the involvement of the two corporals so she could go to Tony with information that he could use, rather than anyone questioning them and them going into hiding. She would make this a priority over the next few weeks and knew it wasn't worth saying anything until she had some worthwhile information. Then, perhaps, she would go through her own chain of command, instead of speaking directly to the police. Whatever she decided, her mission was to ensure she had sufficient information to make them do something about it. The GSM stood up to speak which signalled the end of the presentation and questions.

'Marvellous presentation, gentlemen, and very informative thanks,' he said. 'I'm extremely grateful to you both for taking the time to talk to us all tonight and I know my mess members and guests feel the same.'

On cue there were murmurs of, *'Hear, hear'*, and some enthusiastic mess members banged too vigorously on the table. A look from the GSM stopped this behaviour instantly.

'Please now avail yourselves of our hospitality and enjoy the food, drink and company. There's no organisation on earth better than the British military Warrant Officers and Sergeants Mess…' The MA interrupted the GSM with a little cough and gave him a questioning look which caused the general to guffaw and many mess members to laugh politely.

Mouse watched Tony as he made his way back to his seat. She intended to confront him about the police who he had allocated to follow her. It was over the top and there was no need for it, under the circumstances. They hadn't seen each other socially since their disastrous date night and that must have been clear for all to see and any perceived interest in her must surely have lessened now.

'Well done,' she said. 'That was really good.'

'Thanks, Mouse,' he replied, and said the same to the others around him who were genuinely interested in what had been said.

The seafood medley starter arrived and colleagues around them kept asking questions, so Mouse was able to sit quietly and observe. Not a lover of seafood, she played with her food, picked out a few prawns to eat, but left the rest. The waiters topped up the glasses every time they were less than half empty and she didn't think about how much she was drinking. Having not eaten all day, it went straight to her head and she started to relax.

'Are you okay?' Tony asked when the starter plates were cleared away.

'Fine, thanks.' She let her guard down and could feel the attraction between them. 'I'll be glad when the main course arrives, I'm well hungry.'

'Me too. Are you busy this weekend?'

'Depends on who's asking?'

Laughter from the RAF Sergeant sitting opposite her which reminded both of them that they weren't alone. The Beef Wellington arrived. Mouse hadn't looked at the menu and was disappointed with the standard, unimaginative, Reggy Dinner main course; she expected better from this GSM but guessed that deep down, he was just like the others. She supposed it would be profiteroles for dessert and grabbed a menu card. Yup, absolutely right, they were pleasing the majority with the boring menu as she had suspected. The RAF Sergeant asked Tony how he got his George Cross which piqued her attention.

'It was nothing really.'

'You don't get a George Cross for nothing,' the man replied. 'It's generally awarded for extreme bravery,' he said, addressing Mouse.

'I'm aware of that,' she said, stiffly. 'What happened, Tony, or don't you want to talk about it?'

'A colleague was about to be shot and I put myself in his place, that's all.'

'And?' asked the man opposite.

'And I got shot, twice. It's the same as any of you guys would do and they gave me a medal.'

'Wow, how brave. When was this?' Mouse asked.

'A few years ago, in the Walled City.'

'And you're still in the police and have to go there?' They were all impressed, and Tony took a few seconds to gather his thoughts before responding.

'I was lucky. It could have been any of us but it just happened to be me who took the bullets. It did make me wonder about my mortality, but my choice was to become an office ninja and let it beat me or to carry on and hope it doesn't happen again; I chose the latter.'

Discovering more about this man was fascinating. There were depths there that she hadn't fathomed, and Mouse knew she had been too quick to judge. Some of the other mess members were battle hardened and a few started to share their own war stories. Mouse was only half-listening while trying her best to deal with her conflicting emotions. Having been determined not to let Tony get under her skin, she felt her resolve wilting with each sip of wine. Perhaps she should stop drinking but she was enjoying the atmosphere, the company and the anecdotes and felt happy sitting next to this man, although he had annoyed her. *Let's see what happens,* she thought.

The profiteroles came and went, and the PMC banged his gavel. The talking stopped as all looked to the top table. 'Honoured guests, Sir, fellow mess members. There will now be a ten-minute break to ease springs. Please return to your seats by twenty-two ten hours.'

The others watched as the top table left the dining room then the smokers quickly followed. Mouse was busting for the loo so she made her way to the ladies room. The other four female mess members were there; Hazel, CBF's PA, a petty officer, and two RAF Sergeants.

They checked themselves in the mirrors after using the loos and chatted about the evening. The Sergeants Mess was one of the few places where the queues in the ladies were smaller for women than they were for men.

'That DS is fit looking,' said Hazel. '

'I suppose he is,' said Mouse. 'I hadn't really noticed.'

'Yeah, right. If I wasn't married, you'd have a bit of competition.'

They all laughed. 'We're not together but yeah, I suppose he is easy on the eye.'

'Understatement, Mouse. You want to get in there.' Hazel said, making her way to the door as Mouse followed. One of the RAF Sergeants rolled her eyes at Mouse behind Hazel's back.

'Just coz we're single doesn't mean we're after the first good looking bloke that we see.'

Mouse had the urge to tell her she was widowed, not single, but didn't want a conversation to start about her status and how she felt, so she let it go.

WO1 Sutherland and a Royal Navy Petty Officer were late returning to their seats. As the waiters left the table and the cheese boards arrived with the biscuits and grapes, the PMC banged his gavel again and all were silenced. 'Honoured guests, Sir, fellow mess members, pray silence for Major General Patterson, Commander British Forces Hong Kong and Major General Brigade of Gurkhas.'

Everyone clapped politely as the general stood and he waited for everyone to quieten down before speaking.

'Firstly, I would like to thank the GSM for inviting us here tonight. The Warrant Officers and Sergeants Mess is the backbone of the British military establishment and it's always an honour to be a guest in this marvellous establishment.

'Tonight is both a happy and sad occasion. Warrant Officer Class One Oliver Archibald Pickles leaves…'

There were sniggers and the general stopped talking. The GSM whispered something to the PMC who stood up and banged his gavel.

'As you find the GSM's name so amusing, Sergeant Laurence, perhaps you'd like to donate two bottles of port to the mess for us all to enjoy later on tonight?'

'Yes, Sir,' said a disgruntled Sergeant Laurence, having been the only one caught laughing at hearing the GSM's full name.

The general coughed and continued. Everyone stopped muttering and he continued with his speech about the GSM's distinguished career. While acting as if the general had her full attention, Mouse discreetly looked at other mess members. Despite the general being a fine orator and adding a few amusing anecdotes where members chuckled or laughed as appropriate, many people were quickly bored with speeches. He didn't drag it out for too long and concluded.

'So to go back to my first point. The sad occasion is that you lose one of the best, if not *the* best, Garrison Sergeant Major I have ever had the pleasure of serving with. But your loss is our gain and I look forward to dining with soon-to-be Captain Pickles in the Officers Mess.'

Everyone clapped as the general sat down, then the PMC banged his gavel and introduced the GSM who stood.

'Thank you for your kind words, Sir.' The GSM addressed the general first, then continued, 'Extra port for everyone tonight.' He nodded to WO1 Sutherland, then to the Petty Officer who Mouse didn't know, and finally to Sergeant Laurence. 'Mr Fong,' he said, and the Mess Manager placed four bottles of port on the table in front of the GSM – the fines for their late return to the table and for Sergeant Laurence's inappropriate laughing.

'I'm both sad and elated to stand before you tonight. After twenty years' service and at the pinnacle of my career, I'm moving to the dark side.'

Genuine laughter came from the mess members who settled down shortly after as the GSM continued talking. He was less entertaining than the general and Mouse risked a sneaky look at Tony while trying to zone out from the boring speech. She didn't usually go for blonde men, but he was the exception. He was dark blonde and his eyes were dark blue. She remembered that his eyes had the ability to sparkle when he found something amusing, and they were doing that now. Probably because he looked quickly at her and had caught her studying him when she should have been paying attention to the GSM. *Damn!* thought Mouse, feeling herself blushing.

The speech over, the diners clapped, and there followed the toasts, first to HRH The Queen, followed by absent friends, and then came the regimental marches where members were required to stand to their own.

Not long after the gavel banged, the top table were allowed to leave, and the junior mess member was required to entertain the rest of them with his jokes. Fortunately for those remaining, the newly promoted sergeant was both confident and funny and had to be told to stop a while later so the remaining members could join the seniors in the bar.

Mouse and Tony stayed together. Her earlier plan was to introduce him to other mess members so she would only have to spend the minimum amount of time with him. But that resolve had disappeared around about the same time as the third glass of wine, which had been a little while earlier, and Mouse was enjoying his company. She hiccupped and excused herself and they both laughed. The attraction between them was obvious, and Tony was enjoying himself, being hosted by the crazy Welshwoman. His plan had worked, and he hoped to be able to come clean about it a few months down the line, if everything else worked out.

They were chatting in a group with four other people and Mouse was leaning on Tony to keep her balance when DCI Carpenter and the GSM came over.

'It's time for us to leave, Skip.' The DCI addressed Tony.

'Sergeant Halfpenny,' said the GSM and Mouse tried to act as sober as she could. The DCI, DS, GSM and Mouse made their way to the lift lobby.

'Thanks for a superb night, Ollie,' said the DCI. 'This place won't be the same without you.'

'I'd like to add my thanks,' said Tony. 'Excellent food, company and entertainment. It's been a fabulous night. Good luck in your new role too.'

'Thanks, and always a pleasure.' The men shook hands then the GSM added. 'Sergeant Halfpenny, escort our guests off HMS Tamar then return to the mess.'

'Yes, Sir.' She replied then covered her mouth in an attempt to quieten her hiccups. The GSM gave her a dirty look.

'It's the grapes, Sir. They always have this effect on me, and I shouldn't eat them.'

'Of course it is.'

There was a ping sound signalling the arrival of the lift and the three got in. 'Saved by the bell.' Mouse thought she whispered as the lift doors started to close, then giggled to herself when she saw the stern look on the face of the GSM. The DCI and Tony tried not to laugh while the GSM could still hear.

'I think we can find our own way ashore,' said the DCI and Mouse laughed again. It was weird that HMS Tamar was a building and some people referred to leaving her as *going ashore* when they were already on dry land.

'No, Sir. I insist. And if it's discovered I haven't done as ordered, you know where I'll be without a paddle.'

'Very well.'

'Good night, Guv,' Tony said to his boss as they left the building. 'It would be ungentlemanly of me not to escort Sergeant Halfpenny safely back to the mess.'

'Are you sure?' His boss gave him a weary look, and both knew he wasn't asking about escorting Mouse back to the mess.

'Absolutely certain, Guv.'

Mouse didn't argue. 'Floor twenty-two,' she said when they entered the lift. Tony pressed the button and their eyes locked. Her heart felt like it would burst out of her chest and, unable to hold back any longer, she leant into him and their lips met. Mouse felt the surge of electricity shoot from her stomach to her thighs and all areas in between. The lift stopped and they drew apart as the doors opened and made their way to her room. Her hand was shaking, and Mouse couldn't get her key in the lock, so Tony took it off her, opened the door and she fell inside. He caught her before she hit the deck.

Safely in her room, she led him to her bed and put her arms around him. They kissed and Mouse pulled Tony onto the bed with her.

Tony sat up. 'Are you sure about this, Mouse? Is it really what you want?' he asked, knowing she was drunk and trying to do the right thing.

'Absolutely,' she whispered. Mouse sat up and started to nuzzle his ear before she hiccupped, then laughed, self-consciously.

'Shall I get you some water?' Tony asked, before making his way to the small fridge.

Tony was less than a minute getting her a glass of water, but Mouse was already flat out on the bed, eyes closed and breathing softly. He stripped her down to her underwear, removed the quilt from underneath her and covered her with it. She hadn't been feeling sick beforehand, so he felt safe to leave. He closed the door quietly on his way out, hoping now that the ice was broken, she would be as friendly the following day when she was sober as she had been with a belly full of booze.

Mouse was mortified when she woke with a banging headache the following morning and discovered she was only wearing her underwear. She never went to bed dressed just in bra and knickers and couldn't remember everything that had happened the night before. Deciding a shower would clear her head, she spent an age under the hot water and felt better when making her way back to her room. Then a memory hit her. She had snogged Tony in the lift, and again in her room, and hadn't gone back to the mess as ordered by the GSM. She blamed the alcohol for lowering her defences, but instead of feeling ashamed, she just felt a little embarrassed. Knowing the attraction was still there between them, she wondered what to do. As she towel-dried her hair, the phone rang. She picked up the receiver, hoping the GSM was too hungover to give her a bollocking or punishment today.

'Sergeant Halfpenny, hello.'

'Good morning you mad Welshwoman, well it's only just still morning. How are you feeling today?'

'Slightly better now that I managed to drag myself to the shower. And you?'

'Only a little worse for wear, Mouse. How do you fancy a coffee followed by a leisurely stroll somewhere quiet, then perhaps lunch?'

'Somewhere quiet in Hong Kong, Tony? And you call me mad!' They both laughed. 'But yes, I'm up for that.'

'Shall we say thirty minutes?'

They agreed to meet and hung up. Mouse felt an overwhelming relief that they would be able to discuss everything face to face, rather than on the phone.

They met in Central Plaza, not far from Victoria Harbour. Mouse still felt a little awkward when she saw Tony, but he put paid to that by greeting her with a hug, and when they broke, by asking, 'Are you okay?'

'I am now,' she replied. 'Sorry about last night.'

'No need to apologise, Mouse. I'm glad my plan worked.'

'Plan?'

'I want to be straight with you from the off. My Guv is a good mate of your GSM and knew he was leaving. I suggested it might be a good time to remind military personnel of what goes on here behind the scenes. He put it to your GSM, who agreed.'

'Fair enough.'

'That's not all of it.'

'So, I'm guessing you asked for me to host you? Or is that me being vain?'

Tony chuckled. 'You should be the detective and yes, spot on.'

'I don't know whether to be annoyed or flattered.'

'Can we go for flattered? I don't want this date to end before it's begun, and it would be good not to have any drama. You must know I'm really attracted to you, Mouse, I…'

'I suppose you didn't have much choice as I wouldn't answer your calls,' she interrupted. 'I'm not annoyed, Tony and I'm glad to see you. I was a bit full on last night. I could blame the drink but I only kiss people if I want to, whether I've had a drink or not.'

'Well that's good to know. Shall we get a coffee? I've checked the timetable and we've got twenty minutes before the next bus to Shek O.'

'Sounds good to me, but Shek O? Where's that?'

'All will become clear if you let me be your guide for the rest of the day?'

Mouse agreed and after enjoying their delicious cappuccinos, they boarded the bus twenty minutes later.

They passed Causeway Bay, Quarry Bay and Tai Tam Gap on their journey from the Central Region on their way to the rural marine park located at Shek O, at the South Eastern part of Hong Kong Island. The bus ride took forty minutes and Mouse was glad to get off.

'The driver's a bloody maniac,' she said, rubbing her behind as they watched the bus turn around for the return journey. 'My bum's totally numb.'

'Many people come to Hong Kong and only see the touristy and shopping areas. I want you to see all of it, and that includes areas off the beaten track.'

Mouse followed Tony as he walked towards a rocky looking cliff which overlooked a bay. 'That's where we're headed for now,' he said, pointing towards a beach.

'Where is everyone?' she asked.

'I know. Isn't it just great?'

There was a winding pathway further along which was less steep than the cliff, but still splattered with scree in places. It was wide enough for two people and Tony took her hand in case she slipped. She didn't protest, enjoying the warmth of her hand in his.

Fifteen minutes later they were on the beach, looking out at the South China Sea towards one of the Po Toi Islands in the distance. There were a handful of people in surfer gear and one or two families walking along the beach but other than that it was deserted. They walked and talked and walked some more. They left the beach and ascended a less steep path which took them into the village. It was less hectic than the more built up areas of Hong Kong, but still very busy. It was weird how less than a thirty-minute walk away they went from almost wilderness to busy streets teeming with people.

'Hungry?' Tony asked. The long walk and sea air had made Mouse ravenous and she said so. As she ate her noodles, vegetables and chicken and Tony got stuck into his seafood, they people watched and chatted, getting to know each other better.

'So what made you want to join the Army, Mouse? I can't imagine you were a typical recruit?'

'You mean like your average seventeen-year-old girl who wants to be a secretary or work in a shop, Tony?' she smiled sarcastically.

'Okay, fair point, but I didn't mean to be sexist and I think you've read the wrong meaning into my question. I want to know everything about you, that's all.'

'I'm sorry, Tony. It's just that it's sometimes hard being a woman in a man's world. I do the same job as a lot of blokes, but they get paid more and because we can't go fully operational yet, they have more posts available to them with better chances of promotion.'

'It's the same with the police too. Hopefully it'll change, Mouse. I can see you are dedicated to your career and you wouldn't be working for top brass unless you were good at what you do.'

'Aw thanks, that's a lovely thing to say.'

They listened to the sea in companionable silence for a few minutes before Mouse spoke again. 'So, there was a family secret that I discovered. I wanted to get away so I joined the Army. I got engaged to one man and married another. The one I'd been engaged to murdered my husband and our dog, with the help of a woman who hated me. The murderer is no longer with us, thankfully, and the horrible woman is in prison where she can't do anyone else any harm. And now, here I am in Hong Kong all these years later.

'Wow!'

'Wow indeed,' said Mouse, 'and what about you?'

'Well, I am one of twins.'

'Really? Are you identical? Twins fascinate me…'

'It's not like that, Mouse. I was ill when we were born and had to stay in hospital longer than my brother. When my parents were driving home with my brother their car was hit by a drunk driver. They all died and so did the driver and passenger of the other car, so I was brought up by my grandparents.'

'Oh, Tony, I'm so sorry. How awful for you.'

'I can't remember exactly when they told me they were my grandparents but it seems like I've always known so they must have told me as soon as I was old enough to understand. All I have of my brother, Philip, is one photo taken in the hospital, but there are lots of my parents.'

Mouse reached for his hand across the table and they held hands in silence, contemplating what could have been and what the future now held for them both.

Before she knew it, the day had disappeared and Mouse was surprised to discover it was almost seven o'clock.

'The time bandits have stolen some of today I reckon,' she said on the bus back into Central Region. 'It's just flown by.'

'I know. But it doesn't have to end yet. Not unless you want it to?'

'I'm in no hurry, Tony. What do you fancy doing?' she asked. He gave her a questioning look and Mouse felt herself reddening as they both laughed.

'Err, would you like to come back to mine?'

'Good idea.' They both knew what was going to happen and were impatient to reach their destination. After alighting the bus, they held hands and rushed to Tony's flat in the Mid-Levels. Keeping hold of each other, they rushed through the crowds, raising their arms high in the air to reach over the heads of those who were too slow to get out of their way and leaving stunned faces in their wake.

Overcome by desire in the lift, Tony pulled Mouse to him and kissed her. She didn't hold back, and they were lost in each other until they felt something in the silence. The doors had opened, and two men stood smirking at them.

Mouse disengaged herself and went to walk out of the lift.

'This isn't my floor,' Tony said.

'Clearly not, mate,' one of the men replied in an Australian accent. 'No need to ask you if you're having a good weekend, Tone?' The two men laughed.

'So far so good,' Mouse smiled sweetly. 'I think you can wait for the next lift.' She pressed a button and gave them a little wave as the doors closed.

They held hands while waiting for the lift to reach the destination, then entered his flat and carried on where they'd left off.

The last man who'd touched her breasts had been Guy and that felt like another lifetime ago. As Tony caressed a nipple, Mouse groaned as a surge of heat hit her stomach, thighs and her pleasure centre. He pressed his body into hers and she groaned again, feeling his hardness through her jeans. They stripped urgently and explored every part of each other's body. His chest was almost bare, and Mouse revelled in the taste of his small nipples. She began licking and kissing each of them before moving her tongue further down his body. His fingers probed inside her until she couldn't stand it any longer. She pulled herself astride him, guiding herself onto his penis and moving slowly up and down, all the time watching his face as he kissed her and fondled her breasts.

When she'd wondered about making love with another man, Mouse had thought Guy would be on her mind. But he wasn't. She'd made her peace and it was time to move on. A primal lust took her to heights she hadn't reached in years and when she orgasmed, she cried out in pure pleasure.

'Wow. Just wow!' Tony panted as Mouse collapsed onto him, still joined together. She smiled and rolled off him, then nestled her head underneath his chin. Her old life was over, and this was a new beginning. It was a release in more ways than one and she felt tears roll down her cheeks.

'Hey, it's okay,' Tony said, stroking her hair.

'You're the first since Guy and it's all a bit…'

Mouse sobbed.

'I'm honoured, Mouse and I know it's going to take time but…'

'No, it's not like that. I've been living in limbo now for God knows how long. Guy wouldn't want me to die with him, he'd want me to live my life, and I'm crying because I've said a final goodbye to my past. I'm ready to move on, Tony.'

He wrapped her in his arms, and they were both smiling as he realised he didn't want to live another day of his life without this woman in it.

Chapter 9 – Love and Loss

The rest of that day and night was spent making love, sleeping and snacking. Sunday evening came too soon, and Mouse sighed, knowing she had to make a move. She hadn't readied her kit for the week ahead and her military mentality wouldn't allow her to leave it to do on a day to day basis.

'Shall we walk back and have something to eat on the way?' Tony asked, and Mouse wondered if now would be a good time to speak to him about her concerns regarding the Gurkha and Chinese corporals. She decided to leave it until she had something concrete to tell him, not wanting anything to spoil their weekend together. She also knew she should tell him that she knew he had somebody following her, but that could wait until later too.

'Good idea. I've worked up quite an appetite today.'

They kissed, which led to more love making and it was thirty minutes later when they eventually left Tony's flat.

After some delicious ribs in *Dan Ryan's,* they headed towards HMS Tamar. 'Busy week for me,' Tony reminded Mouse after their final kiss outside the building. 'But can you do dinner on Thursday night?'

'Of course.' That would give her some time to get further information and she'd share her suspicions with him then.

Back in the real world in the office on Monday, the brigadier reminded her that Captain Gurung's funeral was to take place the following day.

'The Provost Marshal has released the body so the family can say goodbye and start the grieving process.'

So he was capable of expressing empathy.

'My wife will come to the office with me tomorrow, Mouse, and we'll leave from here.'

'Yes, Sir,' she said, knowing that meant she'd need to keep Mrs Harding-Brown amused until they left at ten o'clock to go to the funeral. Mrs Harding-Brown was a pleasant and thoughtful woman, so that wasn't a problem. Thinking of the dead captain's family, Mouse wondered if his wife had known anything about his dodgy dealings. *Probably not*, she thought. A lot of men didn't share their work life with their wives, and that also went for Gurkhas as far as she could make out. So she had no reason to believe it was any different for Captain Gurung's wife.

Mouse knew if she was to venture into the Walled City again, she would need help. She hadn't been out to dinner with Alice for a few weeks so decided to phone her to see if they could arrange to meet. She wanted to check out the place she'd seen the two men go into, and although Alice had drawn a little map for her, thought she might need her help to get there. She made a decision that she would share the information she already had but would hopefully be able to get more with a little help from her friend. Alice was busy at lunch time so she called her at home that evening.

'Fancy meeting up one night this week? Tomorrow or Wednesday? It would be good to have a catch up.'

'I'm really sorry, Mouse, I'm only free on Thursday this week,' Alice responded.

'They work you hard in that place, don't they?'

'One of the disadvantages of being a business owner, I guess. Shall we say Thursday then?'

'Actually, I have a date on Thursday.'

'Oooh, tell me more. Who's the lucky man.'

'I'll tell you more when I see you, which looks like it won't be until next week. That's if you can fit me in?'

'Of course. How about next Tuesday? Do you want to come here, or shall we meet somewhere on my way home?'

They arranged to meet in the Bull and Bear and hung up. Mouse decided to speak to Tony on Thursday night, no matter that she had little evidence to substantiate her suspicions. She trusted her gut instinct and knew the two unlikely soldiers were partners in crime. She just had to get someone to prove it. She would also share the fact that she knew he had arranged for her to be followed. Tony had been honest with her and the least she could do was reciprocate. Saying that, Mouse knew he wasn't able to share information about his informants, so decided not to push him on that score.

Thursday dragged and Mouse was relieved and excited when she left work and started to get herself ready to meet Tony. They had spoken on the phone every day and he was busy on a case in work so some had been brief conversations, but tonight she had him all to herself. On her way back from the showers, she opened her door to a ringing phone.

'Hi, Sergeant Halfpenny.'

'It's me, Mouse.'

'Hi, Tony I didn't expect your call. I'm just getting ready now. Is everything okay?'

'I'm really sorry, darling, but something's come up and I have to work tonight. There's been major developments on a case we're working on.'

'Ah, I see.' She tried to hide her disappointment, knowing this could happen at any time.

'Okay then. Well good luck with it and I'll see you when I see you.'

'Hopefully mid-week, Mouse. But I'll phone you tomorrow.'

'I hope whatever it is goes well and good luck with it, Tony.'

'Thanks, Mouse. Love you.' He hung up before she could reply, and she looked at the receiver. He'd said the *L* word and hadn't given her a chance to respond. She didn't feel let down by him postponing their date, instead she felt like someone had put a cuddly blanket around her and given her a huge mug of hot chocolate. Safe and loved and secure in the knowledge that she loved him too and could trust this man. She planned to tell him how she felt the next time they spoke, but in the meantime, she wanted to tell Alice all about him and she wanted to help him solve another case. She picked up the phone. Mouse was about to give up but Alice answered on the tenth ring.

'I know it's short notice but my date's had to cancel so…'

'Oh, Mouse, I'm so sorry. There'll be others.'

'No it's not like that. He's a busy man and has to work. It's just his line of work, Alice, but this is the real thing. We love each other and it's serious.'

'Fantastic! I'm so happy for you both.'

'Thanks. I want to tell you all about it. I know it's short notice but are you still free tonight?'

'I'm really sorry Mouse but business has to come first. Dongmai is ill and I have to work now.'

'Oh, okay.'

'I'm sorry. Hopefully next week if she's better.'

Mouse tried to hide her disappointment for the second time that night. She didn't want her friend to feel guilty.

'Yes, next week. Call me when you're free and I'll try to be too.'

Her head was buzzing too much to want to stay in so Mouse decided to do a bit of investigation on her own. She changed into light jeans and a t-shirt and took the wig she'd bought out of her wardrobe. The silky black hair made her look like a local, at least from behind and although taller than most Chinese women, she thought she'd be able to pass for one at a glance. In fact, she was counting on it. She took the wig off, shook her hair back into place and left her room.

After leaving the MTR, she went into the nearest busy restaurant and entered the ladies' room. It was filled with a mix of South East Asian, European and a few African-looking women, who were all in groups or couples, and while she waited her turn, she tried to work out which languages were being spoken. Cantonese, obviously. She thought she recognised Dutch. A Chinese woman and a European were conversing in English and she hadn't a clue what the African language was. Mouse took the wig out of her bag and propped the compact mirror up against the toilet cistern. She used the mirror to put it on as best she could, then flushed the chain, went outside and washed her hands, and adjusted the wig so it looked more realistic. Other women were fiddling with their hair, so she didn't look out of place. She had a flashback to a time in Holland when she'd dressed in a disguise and managed to evade those following her at the railway station. She chuckled out loud and one woman gave her a strange look before hurriedly leaving the ladies' room. There was nobody following her today, so this was a precaution for Mouse before entering that den of iniquity aka, the Walled City.

Mouse planned on surprising Alice at her café, but it was she who was in for a surprise.

The only way she could allay her terrible sense of direction was to memorise the map on the rough sketch that Alice had drawn for her. She'd looked at it over and over again and was convinced she could find her way to Alice's café. She also hoped she could find her way to the building she had seen the men disappear into on that previous occasion. She didn't have a clue what she would do when she found it but that didn't occur to her. As she entered the Walled City, she was too busy concentrating on going the right way, that she failed to notice the man following her.

Mouse approached the café and stopped short when she saw who was in there. Dongmai, Alice's co-owner was serving behind the counter and was therefore not off sick. This was only one of the observations that made her pull up short; the other was the fact that Alice was talking to a man, and that man was Tony. Not sure how to proceed, she watched for a few seconds, trying to decide whether to enter the café and ask them both what was going on, or to carry on, on her own. Tony looked towards the door and Mouse instinctively ducked out of the way before he could see her. He then disappeared from sight, together with Alice.

She turned and started walking in the direction of where she thought the building was where the two corporals had entered last time she was in the Walled City. Around the corner she stopped; she was certain she could see anyone going in or out of the café, but they couldn't see her. Her mind was working overtime as it tried to work out why Tony would be in Alice's café, and she came up with two possible scenarios. Either they were seeing each other as friends or lovers, or it was something to do with work. She knew Alice loved her husband, and although they hadn't known each other for long, Mouse was convinced that Alice wouldn't be unfaithful to Neil. Something wasn't right about this and she now felt fairly certain that Alice was one of Tony's informants and kept him abreast of what went on within the Walled City. She wondered if Alice had told Tony anything about their discussions. *So if she is a grass,* thought Mouse, *what information is she passing to him and should I go and see them both and tell them about my suspicions?* She immediately decided against it. If either had wanted her to know, they would have told her, and she didn't want Tony or Alice, especially Tony, to think she was following him. He would think she was some sort of crazy stalker woman and that wouldn't do.

Mind made up, Mouse went into the nearest grocery shop for a look around. There were few people in the drinks aisle and she took Alice's rough drawing out of her jeans pocket. Pretending she was checking a shopping list, she studied the route to the building she was looking for, and when satisfied, returned the paper to her pocket. Then she picked up a can of coke, paid at the till and left the shop. The man following her spoke into his radio then walked past Mouse in the opposite direction. The man on the other end of the radio checked the magazine and attached it to his pistol before putting the pistol in his inside jacket pocket. He left his small room and ran down two flights of stairs. As he left the building, he saw the woman turn the corner and memorised her blue jeans, black jacket and the gait of her walk. He kept her at a distance in front of him, ensuring that he never lost sight of her.

Mouse walked through the winding backstreets heading in the direction of what she had come to think of as the forbidden building. Adrenaline surged through her and although she was frightened of what she might encounter, she was buzzing and felt alive. Her senses were on high alert and she noticed everything her eyes could take in, which didn't include anything behind her.

Meanwhile, back at the cafe, Tony watched through the dangly curtain where he and Alice had gone to hide, and saw Mouse disappear around the corner.

'She doesn't know we've seen her,' he told Alice.

'What will you tell her?'

'The truth, eventually, but in the meantime, we need to get moving.' He nodded towards two men in suits who were approaching the café. Alice looked while Tony removed his radio from his pocket.

'Skip to Bravo, over.'

'Send,' said RSM Wardson

'They're approaching the café. Move now, over.'

'Roger and out.'

The RSM and his four-man team appeared seemingly out of nowhere and two tackled each suited Chinese man. One of the suits managed to get a hand in his pocket but was stopped before he could reach his gun. A few passers-by glanced at the skirmish but then went about their own business as both men were escorted roughly into Alice's café. People in the Walled City knew it was better not to be seen or get involved in police, or anything else that didn't involve them for that matter.

The men were handcuffed, and Alice was ordered to pull the shutters down. She did so, secure in the knowledge that she was safe – for the time being anyway.

The café backed onto a small lane and another team of Hong Kong plain-clothed police were waiting at the back door, ready to escort the prisoners to their Police Station.

This part of the operation complete, Tony spoke to Alice and another woman in the café. Dressed in jeans and t-shirt and wearing an apron, she looked like any other café worker, but was one of his undercover operatives.

'So far, so good. Kay-Lee. Get onto the station and get an escort for you and Alice. Take her to a safe house until you hear from me. Get her husband to join you too.'

'Yes, Skip. What about you?'

Tony's radio came to life and he put his hand up while he took the call.

'Shit!' they heard him say, and waited to hear what was happening.

'Mouse has just entered 14K's main building. Get Alice out of here and I'll be in touch when this is over.'

'Good luck, Skip,' she said, but he'd already disappeared onto the street.

Tony ran as fast as he could without a care for who might have been on his tail. Mouse was in serious danger and she probably didn't even know it.

*****

Mouse took a deep breath and entered the building. It was quiet and she could almost hear the blood pumping far too quickly through her veins. Like many of the less upmarket buildings she had encountered in Hong Kong, the stairwell was cluttered with debris. In this one, some of it was moving in this one and by the time she had ascended the first three flights of stairs, checked for any activity on each of the floors and listened outside doors to no avail, she decided to take the lift. Her plan was to stop on each floor, have a look around for anything obvious, then move on to the next one. She had no idea what she was looking for but hoped to see or hear something that would help to convince the police and the military chain of command that her two *suspect* corporals were up to no good.

She heard a couple arguing inside one flat and the sound of televisions coming from most of the others. She hadn't yet encountered anyone and by the time she reached the tenth floor she was already bored. She changed her plan, deciding to go up to the roof, have a nosey around there, and then make her way back downstairs. She pressed number twenty-eight, the highest number displayed on the buttons and waited as the lift ascended slowly. It came to an abrupt stop at floor fifteen and the doors opened. A man pulled open the outside cage door and entered the lift. He glanced at her, smirked, pressed number twenty-seven and turned towards the lift doors, facing away from Mouse. Dressed in a black suit with a tie and white shirt she thought he looked out of place in this building. In fact, he reminded Mouse of one of the men who Tony had arranged to follow her. He also reminded her

165

of the triads, and she wondered why they all chose to dress the same. *So they fit in with their surroundings,* she thought, assuming that everybody in the area knew these snazzy dressers were criminals and would give them a wide berth. It was a flaming cheek and she decided to tell him so.

'Excuse me?'

The man turned, a look of surprise on his face.

'I know what you're up to you know, you can't fool me.'

He laughed then shrugged his shoulders. Mouse thought he looked quite bemused so must have been a good actor.

'I know that Tony has sent you to follow me.' she said in precise English, clear and loud. 'And I know you can understand English so the game's up.'

He said something in Chinese then moved closer as if he was about to do or say something else. The lift pinged and stopped, and the man sneered back a laugh as he exited the lift.

What the hell was that about? she wondered before stepping out of the lift.

Up here, there weren't any corridors to walk along, just a set of stairs right in front of her and she heard raised voices coming from that direction. The argument was taking place in both English and Chinese. The English voice sounded familiar. She tried to be as quiet as she could, going up the metal stairs, but her heel clanged on one of them and silence fell, the shouting stopped and Mouse thought better of her decision to go to the roof. She turned, deciding to get the hell out of Dodge. But the man who had been in the lift with her was standing at the bottom of the stairs and he didn't look best pleased. If the choice was trying to rush past one or being in a bit of trouble with more than one up on the roof, she would go for the former. The choice was taken out of her hands however when the man put a hand in his jacket and withdrew a gun. He said something in Chinese and gestured with his pistol for her to go up the stairs.

'Oh shit,' she whispered under her breath. Even though she knew there was no way out of this situation, and with her mind still working overtime as she tried to figure out why a colleague of Tony's was pointing a gun at her, she turned and slowly started to climb the stairs. It dawned on her that she was wrong and she was being followed by triads, and not a member of the Hong Kong Police. The realisation made her legs go weak and she almost collapsed on the stairs. Mouse stopped to compose herself and a few seconds later she felt cold metal being thrust into her lower back. It was all she could do not to wet herself. It didn't matter now if her feet made a noise but the clank of her shoes on the metal stairs seemed amplified and she wondered if everyone in the Walled City could hear her. She got moving again and rushed up the stairs, trying to get away from feeling the cold of the weapon, but knowing he was right behind her.

At the top of the stairs he pushed her forward. The two men she'd heard were talking now, and to her surprise, one of them was Earl Cartwright. She recognised the other as the man he had met in the London pub, and the same one she had seen with his bodyguards, when she was in The Hilton that night with Tony. She noticed the bodyguards weren't with him now, but the Chinese and Gurkha corporals were, both holding guns at their sides.

'Earl?'

'How the hell did you get yourself involved in this, Welshie?' he asked.

But Mouse didn't answer. She was too busy watching the other man take a gun out of his jacket.

'No,' shouted Earl, putting a hand in his own jacket.

The Gurkha NCO lifted his gun and aimed it at Earl without hesitation. Their leader shouted something, and Mouse watched in horror as she heard a deafening bang and Earl was blown off his feet.

Earl groaned then was deathly still as a puddle of blood started to form around him. As she watched the big Chinese man aim his gun at her, Mouse heard a sound from behind. She turned her head to see Tony, two uniformed policemen and RSM Wardson aiming their guns in the direction of the big Chinese man. Her world went silent, except for the noise of her blood pumping through her veins, which was now almost deafening.

In a moment of clarity, Mouse knew she wasn't ready to spend eternity with Guy. She loved Tony, had a life to live, a man to love and she intended to do anything she could to avoid the bullets.

She heard a noise and her brain told her the first round had whizzed past her.

She wasn't so lucky with the second.

'Down!' Tony shouted, but she was too late. She heard one of the men behind her hit the deck but also felt a sharp pain where the round hit her flesh. Mouse lost consciousness before hitting the ground.

Chapter 10 – Wet and Windy Wales

It was windy and wet. The sort of rain that drizzled constantly and seemed to find its way right into your bones. Graham, his father, and Tony were among the six bearers who brought her coffin into the Crematorium Chapel. Elaine and Spike had asked to be bearers, and although it was unusual for women to be coffin bearers, the family agreed, knowing that it would have been what Mouse had wanted. Then the family took their places in the front pew, next to Grace, Elfie and Mouse's mother who were all crying quietly. They didn't even have the closure that came with looking at her body and saying farewell, such was the extent of her injuries. The friends joined Cathy in the row behind.

Majors Best and Drake were there from her unit in Germany, standing next to Brigadier Harding-Brown and his wife. Wanting to be seen to do the right thing, Q Johnson had decided to attend and was standing towards the rear with Mr Walker. She looked longingly at the back of the brigadier, wondering what might have been if Mouse coffin hadn't ruined it for them.

Alice and Neil Mitchum had decided to attend the funeral before departing for Neil's two-year posting to the Falkland Islands. It wasn't somewhere Alice would have chosen to go but she knew they would be safe there until the heat died down. Neil was standing next to Captain Wardson who they met at the funeral and Alice did a good job of pretending she didn't know him.

'Captain Wardson is posted to the Falklands too, love.' Neil said to his wife. They shook hands and the newly promoted captain, who had been decorated for his undercover work as a SIB RSM, knew his job of keeping these two safe in such an isolated location would be a doddle. All new arrivals could be traced and anyone of a different ethnicity would stand out like a sore thumb.

It was a non-religious type service with a fitting eulogy from Graham. Nobody laughed when the coffin disappeared on the conveyer belt to the sound of the Trammps Disco

Inferno on the old-fashioned cassette player owned by the undertakers. Mouse had written a will after her husband had died and had specified the music she wanted at her funeral should the worst happen, and as far as her family were concerned, it couldn't get any worse.

The raw emotion of her family had affected Tony and he didn't need to pretend as he cried with them, even if some of those tears were brought on by guilt.

He hoped they would be able to forgive him with the passage of time.

Chapter 11 – Not as it Seems

Tony immersed himself in his work during the following weeks. He was working on the family tree of Corporal Wong. The NCO would have been charged with the murder of Captain Gurung had he not received a deadly bullet in the chest from one of Tony's team. The fact that his cousin, the waiter found dead in the Sergeants Mess in Germany, had been murdered by the triads did not excuse the fact that he was a member of the 14K Triads and had also been involved with the British Army personnel who smuggled gold from Hong Kong to Nepal and the UK. Tony knew there was enough evidence to have put the man away for a very long time. As it was, the Hong Kong Police had saved a lot of tax-payers' money. The phone on his desk rang and he looked at the number displayed on it.

'Yes, Guv,' he said as he picked up, then shortly after, made his way into his boss's office.

'Well done on this case, Skip,' said DCI Carpenter. 'I know it can't have been easy for you.'

Easier than you'll ever know, thought Tony as his determination to get the bastards put away had been the one thing that kept him sane since the shooting. There was a cold knot in his gut, and he felt some satisfaction that the smuggling ring had now been stopped and a number of personnel, both military and triads, had been charged and were in prison, pending their trials. The Gurkha Corporal was one of these after his suicide attempt had failed. If Captain Gurung hadn't been so greedy, he might still be alive and in the company of his prison mates.

The DCI's voice interrupted his thoughts. 'You are to receive another commendation from the Governor of Hong Kong for your bravery and have been recommended for public recognition from the UK. Congratulations, we're all very proud of you.'

'Thanks, Guv. It doesn't make much difference though…'

'On the contrary, Skip, it makes one hell of a lot of difference. More people can walk the streets in safety in Hong Kong and many other places, thanks to our team, and more specifically, your work on this case. It might be difficult for you to acknowledge this under the current circumstances, but you should be very proud of yourself.' He held out his hand and shook Tony's vigorously, while Tony failed to show the same level of enthusiasm.

'Moving on,' said the DCI. 'The main focus now is to ensure the safety of her family. Any news?'

'The only news, Guv, is no news. It's been a month and there's no reports of her parents being watched in Wales, or of her brother and his family at his unit near Southampton.'

'Talking of his unit. Does his Commanding Officer...?'

'His CO knows we're keeping a watchful eye on Staff Sergeant Warbutton's family and his inlaws, Gov, but that's all they know and it's working well. There are no reports of any surveillance on them except from our people.'

'Good, let's keep it like that,' the DCI said, looking down and shuffling some papers on his desk. Tony took this as his cue to leave and returned to his office.

*****

The surveillance continued and seven weeks after Mouse Halfpenny's funeral, Tony was satisfied that nobody from the 14K Triads were monitoring any of her family's movements. He gave it another few weeks, wrote a short report for his bosses, then they called off the surveillance units. Six weeks later he received the call that he'd been waiting for. He phoned her brother, told him there was an issue that needed to be resolved regarding his late sister, and to request some leave and get home as soon as possible, when further information would be forthcoming.

'Nobody's in danger and there's nothing to worry about,' he added.

'What's going on?' Graham asked, but the phone was already dead.

172

Graham phoned his RSM and was told to report to his office. 'I need some leave, Sir. It's my…'

'The OC has already approved it, Staff. We'll see you in two weeks.'

Graham left the office totally confused and hurriedly made his way home. He was even more bemused to discover that Grace had received a call and had packed cases for them both.

'What the hell?'

'I'm going on holiday with Nanny and Grandpa, Daddy, while Mummy has her operation.'

'Of course you are, darling,' Graham said to Elfie, giving Grace a questioning look when his daughter wasn't looking.

'Later,' Grace mouthed.

After dropping off Elfie they jumped into the car. 'Why do your parents and Elfie think you're going into a German hospital for specialist treatment, and why were you packed when I got home? What's going on?' he asked after they'd left the house and driven around the corner. Graham stopped the car and turned to his wife.

'Tony called me and said I need to pack for few weeks, and he gave me this address where all will become clear. We're meeting your parents there, apparently. He said to take Elfie to Mum and Dad's and to trust him-and that it's a matter of life and death that we stick to the story he's given us. I've taken a massive leap of faith here, Graham, so you need to tell me what's going on.'

'I need to tell you?' Graham said, as he put the car in gear and pulled off to start their journey towards London. 'You seem to know a lot more than I do. Mouse has been dead less than four months and he wants us all to go on some sort of holiday near London. It's all very strange if you ask me.'

They were both quiet for a few minutes while they thought of his sister and how raw her death still was.

'Why are we trusting a man that we barely know and doing what he's asked us to do?' Grace wondered.

'Two reasons,' said Graham. 'Firstly, he risked his life to try to save hers which means he either loved her or he's very brave. And secondly, when I went to see the RSM to request leave at short notice, he didn't ask me any questions and told me that my leave had already been approved by the OC.'

'Hmm.' Grace tapped her fingers on the dashboard. 'So this Tony is a good guy then. But what swung your decision is that you think maybe the authorisation for you to have leave came from someone higher up than your OC. Is that about right, Gray?'

'Spot on, Grace. I think Tony has something to tell us all. I'm hoping the families of her killers aren't after revenge.'

'Oh my God, Graham, don't say that. We've left Elfie and…'

'No, Grace. I'm wrong. If that was the case, they would have told us to bring Elfie with us. It's not that.'

'Shall we stop and phone your mum and dad?'

'No. Let's get there as soon as we can and see what they know.'

Later that afternoon they arrived at their destination, a hotel in the countryside outside London. His parents were already waiting for them in the reception area and Graham's mother pulled him into a fierce hug as soon as she saw him, her strength outmatching how frail she looked.

'It's good to see you, son,'

'You too, Mam.' He'd seen her once since the funeral but had spoken to her on the phone at least once a week. He tried to hide his shock at the way both of his parents had aged in such a short time. *I guess that's what losing a child does to you*, he thought, and fought to hold back the tears as soon as he saw that both of his parents were crying. He lost that battle.

'I thought Tony would be here,' he said, as soon as he could break free from his mother.

'He's not coming, son,' Graham's father answered. 'But he's sent a car for us and a driver and said there's no point asking the driver anything as he's just taking us to our destination. There is some sort of information about Michelle

that we need to know about and the only way we can find out
more is by doing what he asks.'

'But what information? What could we possibly
benefit from now that she's...'

His mother sobbed again before he could complete
the sentence and his father held her while the tears came,
along with heaving sobs that wracked her whole body. The
staff on the reception desk looked away and Graham held
Grace's hand as they both watched, crying their own silent
tears, knowing they could do nothing to ease the pain of his
parents.

*****

Tony arrived at the hospital and entered the front door. He
walked along the corridors until he saw a door marked 'Staff
only'. There was a keypad to the side of the door and Tony
keyed in the number and heard a click which unlocked the
mechanism. He went through and closed the door behind
him, then walked along a further two corridors until he came
to a lift. There were no buttons to the sides of the lift, but there
was metal panel with a hole in it and next to it a cream
coloured phone was mounted on the wall. Now familiar with
the routine, he picked up the receiver, keyed in a number and
hung up. A uniformed policeman arrived a few minutes later.

'Tony.'

'Dave.' Tony nodded. 'How's it going?'

'Fine thanks,' Dave replied in his Scottish accent. 'No
dramas.'

That was exactly what Tony wanted to hear as he
watched the policeman insert a key into the hole in the metal
panel. The lift arrived shortly after. 'Do you need me to come
with you?' Dave asked.

'No, I'm good thanks.'

The lift descended and Tony disembarked into an
empty corridor in the cellar. This part of the hospital had state
of the art facilities and was not known about by the general
public. He passed a number of private rooms before arriving
at the corridor where a very special person was
accommodated. If the gods of fate were on her side, she would

175

return to full health. He was yet to discover whether there would be any brain damage or any other long-lasting effects from the shooting.

*****

The bright lights were irritating, and nobody was calling her to walk towards them. They shone into her eyes and her head was already pounding.

'Go away,' she thought she said as she tried to lift her hand to cover her eyes, but it came out as gobbledegook and she didn't recognise her own voice.

'She's coming round,' she heard somebody say.

'I'm not dead then,' she whispered. She felt a straw being put to her lips and she sucked. The water was the best thing she'd ever tasted, and Mouse drank until the dryness eased. She tried to keep her eyes open, but it was a struggle and in the end, she gave up. This time she slept a natural sleep, not in the coma that she had been induced into to save her life.

The next time she opened her eyes she wasn't alone.

'You had us a bit worried there,' Tony said. Mouse lifted her hand and he held it.

'I love you, Tony.' The words were out, and she recognised her voice this time and she could also see the love reflected in his eyes.

'I love you too, you crazy woman. I didn't realise how much until I thought you were dead. Don't ever do anything like this again. I've made deals with all the world's gods in the hope that you'd come back to us.'

'Come back to you, what do you mean and where are we? Why does my face feel so tight?'

'Let's get the medics in here to explain that to you.'

'Can I get a mirror first?'

'Not at the moment, Mouse. Your face is covered in bandages and you've had to have lots of surgery.'

'Oh my God! Am I going to be scarred for life? Is it really bad? Will I be stared at and..'

176

'Nothing like that,' he replied and looked to the door as it opened and a woman in a white coat appeared. She smiled kindly at Mouse.

'Hello there. I'm Doctor Randu Chandrey. How are you feeling?'

'Terrified, doctor. Can I see my face?'

Doctor Chandrey sat on the edge of her bed. She first looked at Tony who nodded, then addressed Mouse. 'To save your life we had to perform extensive surgery. One side of your face was almost completely collapsed, along with your nose where the bullet was embedded. We have no idea how the bullet stopped there but had it gone any further you would have most certainly died.'

She's talking to me as if recounting a shopping trip thought Mouse, trying her best to hide her shock. Then she remembered she was covered in bandages, so Doctor Chandrey had no idea of her facial expressions.

'We had to replace your cheekbones and rebuild your nose. To ensure symmetry in your face, we also had to align the other side.'

'I see,' said Mouse, but she didn't.

'Your injuries were life-threatening, so we had to put you in a coma to give your body a chance to recover properly. One hip has been replaced and your broken femur has now mended, so I'm pleased to say that, with some physiotherapy you should be able to get back to a normal life in due course, physically anyway. We can arrange for therapy to help you cope with any mental issues you may have due to the accident and your recovery.'

Mouse didn't like the sound of therapy. It sounded far too American for her liking and as far as she was concerned, she had friends she could talk to if she wanted to discuss the fallout of what had happened.

The doctor smiled. 'Any questions?'

'When can I see my face?'

The doctor gently touched the bandages. 'Another few days and we'll be able to take the bandages off. I'll let you digest what I've just told you now and if you have any further questions, we can address them later. Your recovery is going to be a long process, so I need you to be patient with me. Your family should be here soon, and Tony needs to speak to you before they arrive, so I'll leave you to it.'

'Thanks, doctor,' Mouse said, purely as a politeness reflex. 'So I nearly did die then, no messing?'

'Yes, your heart stopped at least twice. And I'm sorry but this is going to be really hard to hear, but lots has happened since you were shot, and I need to explain before your family arrive.'

'How long have I been out of it, Tony?'

'Just over three months, Mouse. I need you to be brave, sweetheart and to brace yourself.'

'Over three months!' she said, then, 'Why, what's happened?'

'You were caught up in some serious criminal behaviour, Mouse. Earl Cartwright is dead, the son of the leader of the 14K Triads is dead, and so is one of the key military personnel who was involved in the smuggling. Others are in prison and although the 14K chain of command was in disarray, our intelligence suggests they've already made some promotions and are seeking revenge.'

'So Earl died too. Oh no, that's awful. Cathy told me him and her mum were going to get married. Poor Maeve and poor Earl. I know he was a gangster, Tony, but he helped me and Elaine. Life's not fair…'

'I'm sorry you feel like that, Mouse, but he was a gangster and if he hadn't died, there was enough evidence to lock him away for quite some time. If they married, the wedding would have taken place in prison.'

'I'm still sad, Tony. He was like an uncle…'

'I'm sorry, Mouse.'

'I know you're not, Tony…' She tried to smile but her face felt stiff under the bandages. 'I'll have to phone Cathy to tell her I'm sorry…'

'You can't do that…'

'What do you mean I can't do that? Why can't I? You can't tell me…'

'Mouse,' Tony interrupted and held her hand. 'When I said that the triads were seeking revenge, we had to make some hard decisions to ensure your and your family's safety.' He was silent for a few seconds, wondering if the information about her injuries and now this would be too much to take in all in one go.

'Go on.'

Before Tony could carry on there was a noise outside. 'Your security guards are arguing with someone, give me a minute.'

It was too late. They both heard raised voices. *They told me she was dead and I'm her mother for God's sake!'*

'Dead, Tony?' asked Mouse.

The door swung open and her mother flew through it, followed by her father, Graham and Grace.

'Michelle, Michelle, Michelle! You're alive! Thank God and all the angels. MY DAUGHTER IS ALIVE!' Her mum threw herself at Mouse, managing to dislodge two of the wires that were monitoring her vital signs. Alarms added to the general chaos and Doctor Chandrey reappeared, together with two nurses.

Mouse and her mother were hugging each other and the others looked on, all crying. Graham and Grace held each other and her father went to the other side of the bed and held his daughter's hand. When they broke the embrace, it was her father's turn to speak.

'We were told you had perished, love. We had a funeral for you and everything.'

'A funeral?! Was it a good send-off?' Mouse asked, and her visitors managed a wry laugh at such a bizarre question.

'Oh, aye,' said Graham. 'It was a barrel of laughs, Mouse. You would have loved it. All of your friends were there and your boss and his missus from Hong Kong. And all the while you were alive and this bastard here,' he nodded to Tony, 'this bastard here saw the pain and grief we were all going through and let us believe that you had died. I'm going to…'

The nurses saw what was happening and grabbed at Graham before he could land a punch.

'Do you think it was easy for me?' Tony asked as he stood up. 'Deceiving the family of the woman I love and not knowing whether she was going to die or wake up in a vegetative state? I had no choice and we've had surveillance on all of you to ensure your safety. These guys are killers and it was the only way.' He sat back down, deflated and trying to hide his upset from Mouse.

'So what happens now,' Grace asked, while Graham tried his best to calm down.

'There's still a number of loose ends that need to be tied up and certain criminals are still at large, but we're really close. Nobody else can know that your sister is still alive until they're safely behind bars.'

'And how long is that likely to take?' asked her father.

'I can't say exactly but the doctor estimates that Mouse, sorry, Michelle, will be able to travel in about two weeks. Until then, you can spend time with her here. I've arranged for you all to be driven to and from the hotel to the hospital as often as you wish.'

'So we have to go through the palaver of being blindfolded every time we visit?' asked Grace. 'It's a bit James Bond-ish isn't it?'

'I don't care,' said her mother as she squeezed her daughter's hand. 'My girl is alive and is going to be well and that's all that counts.'

'Do I have your word that this will go no further?' Tony asked and they all agreed unconditionally.

Chapter 12 – Luck Island

Three weeks later, two passengers arrived at the airport check in and the man handed over their passports. His bore the name of Philip Wilson-Dryden, and hers, Sonia Snowdon.

The check-in assistant flicked her manicured nails to the photo section of each document and looked firstly at the man. Then she looked at the wheelchair, bent down and addressed the woman. 'Would you mind removing your sunglasses, madam please, so I can verify your identity.' She smiled through her bright red lips.

'Certainly,' the woman answered. She removed her shades and caught a glance of the photograph in her new passport. Still surprised at her new look, she tried not to act it. Her nose was much prettier now and her cheekbones higher. *I almost look like an Eastern European,* she thought.

'Do you need any assistance?' The check-in lady stood upright again and addressed the man. Mouse - no Sonia, she corrected herself - wondered not for the first time why some people treated wheelchair bound people as if they were invisible. The only reason the woman had spoken to her directly was because she had to check her against her passport. Tony, no Philip, had said this might happen and he had been absolutely spot on. She was perfectly capable of walking but had taken his advice and the wheelchair had the opposite effect of drawing attention to her.

'We're fine, thanks. Aren't we, darling?'

She smiled and nodded as she put her sunglasses back on.

The first flight was to Antigua. Once there, they picked up the connection to the British Virgin Islands, then boarded a private jet for the short hop to the privately-owned Luck Island.

'So who knows we're here?' Sonia asked.

'Just the owner who's also in a witness protection programme, my governor and a few others.'

Both exhausted, they spent the next few days acclimatising and catching up on their sleep.

The following morning Sonia was missing when Philip awoke. He dressed in shorts, vest and trainers as quickly as he could and rushed out. Five minutes later he heard her calling to him and removing his trainers he ran into the sea to join her.

'You had me a bit worried there, Sonia, and should you be in the sun?'

'Take a chill-pill, Phil. 'I'm wearing factor fifty and it's only for a few minutes,' she replied, jumping onto his back which forced them both under the water. When they came up for air she dived backwards and floated for a while, before pushing her feet to the sand with a sigh.

'Not a bad job being a body-guard for someone on the witness protection programme,' she said, indicating the area with both arms. 'Not sure about the new name though.'

'Well you said you've always liked the name Sonia and you are Welsh, so…'

'Will we ever be able to go back to our old lives, To…, I mean Phil?'

'I doubt it, darling. We can stay here until the heat dies down, but our old lives could put us and your family in danger.'

They'd already discussed this, and she knew she could see her family, but only under strict supervision until the dangerous criminals were caught. She would miss the Army but was planning a change of career anyway, so could handle that. It would be difficult not being in contact with her friends though, and she voiced her concerns.

'I'll miss speaking to Elaine and Cathy and I feel bad about…'

'Best not to think about it if we can't do anything about it.'

He was right and it wasn't such a bad life. But as much as this place was a paradise, there was no way she could go through her whole adult life without working. She had an idea that would be perfect for her inquisitive mind and incorporate Philip's training and experience.

'Penny for them?' he said.

Sonia decided now wasn't the best time to tell him her plans for the *Snowdon-Wilson Detective Agency.*

She blew him a kiss and dived under the waves.

Acknowledgements

Thanks to my husband Allan, to my fabulous editor Jill Turner and wonderful cover designer Jessica Bell. Thanks also to all my friends for their support especially Julie, Trudy, Su, John, Stephen, Tina, Libby, Lumpi, Craig, Helen and Debbie

Author's Note

Thank you for purchasing this book, I hope you enjoyed reading it as much as I did writing it.

While the characters in this book are purely fictitious, some of the events and places are based on my own knowledge and experience from serving in the British Army. I have had various postings to Germany, two to London and I served in Hong Kong from 1988 to 1991 working firstly as a PA for the Deputy Commander and later, for the Commander British Forces. My husband Allan was a civilian at this time and worked as a Security Guard for the Hong Kong Government, in British Forces Hong Kong. We did get some strange comments from a few people, someone asked Allan why he had allowed his wife to stay in the Army after he had left. One senior NCO's wife told me that, as a woman, I should not be entitled to married quarter accommodation. She was very anti-women in the Army and during the same conversation I managed to convince her that female soldiers whose husbands were civilians were not required to pay income tax. I owned up that I'd been winding her up about three months later, when her husband was fed up of her telling him how unfair life was!

There were instances of gold-smuggling, and a murder within the British military, in Hong Kong during the 1980s, although if you try to Google this information it's very sparse. There is some information on the Army Rumour Service website and a little on this one (towards the end). https://gurkhainquiry.files.wordpress.com/2014/03/exhibit-6-gurkhas-in-the-service-of-the-crown-satyagrah.pdf

I don't know much about triads and any information included in this book has been found by Googling *Hong Kong Triads*.

If you enjoyed the Unlikely Soldiers series, I'd love it if you'd share your experience by writing a review.

You may be interested in my other books:

Beyond Death (The Afterlife Series Book 1)
Beyond Life (The Afterlife Series Book 2)
Beyond Destiny (The Afterlife Series Book 3)
Beyond Possession (The Afterlife Series Book 4)

The Island Dog Squad Book 1 (Sandy's Story) - FREE AT
THIS LINK https://dl.bookfunnel.com/wdh6nl8p08

The Island Dog Squad (Book 2: Another Crazy Mission)
The Island Dog Squad (Book 3: People Problems)

Court Out (A Netball Girls' Drama)

For children:

Jason the Penguin (He's Different)
Jason the Penguin (He Learns to Swim)

Non-Fiction:

Zak, My Boy Wonder

Further information is on my website
https://debmcewansbooksandblogs.com or you can connect
with me on Facebook:
https://www.facebook.com/DebMcEwansbooksandblogs/?r
ef=bookmarks

About the Author

Following a career of over thirty years in the British Army, I moved to Cyprus with my husband to become weather refugees.

I've written children's books about Jason the penguin and Barry the reindeer, and books for a more mature audience about dogs, the afterlife, soldiers and netball players, along with a non-fiction book about a very special boy named Zak.

Court Out (A Netball Girls' Drama)' is a standalone novel. Using netball as an escape from her miserable home life, Marsha Lawson is desperate to keep the past buried and to forge a brighter future. But she's not the only one with secrets. When two players want revenge, a tsunami of emotions is released at a tournament, leaving destruction in its wake. As the wave starts spreading throughout the team, can Marsha and the others escape its deadly grasp, or will their emotional baggage pull them under, with devastating consequences for their families and team-mates?

The Afterlife series was inspired by ants. I was in the garden contemplating whether to squash an irritating ant or to let it live. I wondered whether anyone *up there* decides the same about us and thus the series was born.

'The Island Dog Squad' is a series of novellas told from a dog's point of view. It was inspired by the rescue dog we adopted in 2018. The real Sandy is a sensitive soul, not quite like her fictional namesake, and the other characters are based on Sandy's real-life mates.

'Zak, My Boy Wonder', is a non-fiction book co-written with Zak's Mum, Joanne Lythgoe. I met Jo and her children when we moved to Cyprus in 2013. Jo shared her story over a drink one night and I was astounded, finding it hard to believe that a family could be treated with such cruelty, indifference and a complete lack of compassion and empathy. This sounded like a tale from Victorian times and not the twenty-first century. When I suggested she share her story, Jo said she was too busy looking after both children – especially Zak who still needed a number of surgeries – and didn't have the emotional or physical energy required to dig up the past. Almost fourteen years after Zak's birth, Jo felt ready to share this harrowing but inspirational tale of a woman and her family who refused to give up and were determined not to let the judgemental, nasty, small-minded people grind them down.

I love spending time with Allan and our rescue dog Sandy. I also love writing, keeping fit, and socialising, and will do anything to avoid housework.

www.ingramcontent.com/pod-product-compliance
Lightning Source LLC
Chambersburg PA
CBHW070516160726
48003CB00004B/1582